Cover Copy

Traveling through time…for a Highlander.

Lila MacIan makes a wish upon a sixteenth century charm gifted to her by her missing grandmother, a wish that sends her traveling back into the past and to a warrior her charm has bound her to. With a vicious feud raging between the clans, she withholds her true identity from him, except he's seen her grandmother and now she must do whatever it takes to find her.

Highland warrior Calum MacLean is bound to a woman who holds an identical charm to his. Visions assail him, of the two of them intimately together, and as Lila escapes him for the enemy's land, his soul demands he protect and aid her.

Once Lila is reunited with her grandmother, she discovers she was born in the past to the MacIan laird, Calum's arch enemy. Can she find a way to save the man her soul cries out for…set her past to rights and remain in her true time?

Books by Joanne Wadsworth

The Matheson Brothers Series
Highlander's Desire, Book One
Highlander's Passion, Book Two
Highlander's Seduction, Book Three
Highlander's Kiss, Book Four
Highlander's Heart, Book Five
Highlander's Sword, Book Six
Highlander's Bride, Book Seven
Highlander's Caress, Book Eight
Highlander's Touch, Book Nine
Highlander's Shifter, Book Ten
Highlander's Claim, Book Eleven
Highlander's Courage, Book Twelve
Highlander's Mermaid, Book Thirteen

Highlander Heat Series
Highlander's Castle, Book One
Highlander's Magic, Book Two
Highlander's Charm, Book Three
Highlander's Guardian, Book Four
Highlander's Faerie, Book Five
Highlander's Champion, Book Six
Highlander's Captive (Short Story)

Billionaire Bodyguards Series
Billionaire Bodyguard Attraction, Book One
Billionaire Bodyguard Boss, Book Two
Billionaire Bodyguard Fling, Book Three

Books by Joanne Wadsworth

Regency Brides Series
The Duke's Bride, Book One
The Earl's Bride, Book Two
The Wartime Bride, Book Three
The Earl's Secret Bride, Book Four
The Prince's Bride, Book Five
Her Pirate Prince, Book Six

Princesses of Myth Series
Protector, Book One
Warrior, Book Two
Hunter (Short Story - Included in Warrior, Book Two)
Enchanter, Book Three
Healer, Book Four
Chaser, Book Five

Highlander's Charm

Highlander Heat, Book Three

Joanne Wadsworth

Highlander's Charm
ISBN-13: 978-1-99-003424-4
Copyright © 2014, Joanne Wadsworth
Edited by Penny Barber
First electronic publication: September 2014

Joanne Wadsworth
http://www.joannewadsworth.com

All Rights Are Reserved. No part of this book may be used or reproduced in any manner whatsoever without written permission, except in the case of brief quotations embodied in critical articles and reviews. The unauthorized reproduction or distribution of this copyrighted work is illegal. No part of this book may be scanned, uploaded or distributed via the Internet or any other means, electronic or print, without the author's permission.

PUBLISHER'S NOTE:
This book is a work of fiction. The names, characters, places, and incidents are products of the writer's imagination or have been used fictitiously and are not to be construed as real. Any resemblance to persons, living or dead, actual events, locale or organizations is entirely coincidental. The author does not have any control over and does not assume any responsibility for third-party websites or their content.

Published in the United States of America

First digital publication: September 2014
First print publication: October 2014

Dedication

Writing this book took me on a wonderful journey where I discovered anything is possible. This one is for you, my readers. Let's do some more traveling through time.

Acknowledgements

Huge thanks go to my hubby, Jason, and kiddies, Marisa, Caleb, Cruise and Rocco, an incredibly supportive family who allow me so much time to write. My love for you is endless.

I also have the most amazing editor, Penny Barber. The absolute best.

For my readers, I can't thank you enough for joining me, and taking this journey to where imagination and magic soar.

The Fortuneteller

Within the forests of Ardnamurchan, 1569.

Blazing bright, a falling star streaked across the night sky. The earth shook, and deep within the woods, the fortuneteller gripped her walking stick and staggered to her feet. Her campfire sizzled and sparked, and the small creatures of the night scuttled away through the underbrush.

Eyes closed, she reached out with her senses. A portal had opened between times and displaced two souls. Both had been born under a falling star, one mere moments ago, and the other, many years.

Aye, a grandmother and her newborn granddaughter, both with silver eyes giving evidence of their special birth, as it had with hers.

The magic of the stars moved through their blood, only the grandmother had made a pleading wish for the bairn, and it had taken the two of them through time and far from Scotland. They would not return to this place until they once again stood on the land of their birth and made another wish.

Looking deep inside her mind, she searched for aid. A vision shimmered to life. A lad of seven roamed the woods on the neighboring Isle of Mull, his gaze lifted to the sky. Calum too had seen the falling star and sensed the disruption in time, though his eyes held no trace of silver.

Tears streaked the boy's cheeks as he whispered the newborn girl's name. Lila. She was his, and she'd been taken from him, not that he understood how or why.

The fortuneteller shoved her braided gray hair over her shoulder, then from amongst her wrist-full of silver bangles, removed two brass charms. As kin to the grandmother and her grandchild, 'twas her duty to set all that had occurred back to rights. If needed, she would cross time itself to ensure they returned to their homeland.

She handed the charms to her son as he sat across the fire, instructing him to inscribe Calum and Lila's names upon them.

These two pieces would bind them together as their souls already did. Though Lila was special. She would be able to draw on the magic deep within her to make wishes, ones that would come true when she was at her most desperate, as her grandmother had been this eve.

Time itself would not keep Calum and Lila apart.

She'd make certain of it.

The Charms

Duart Castle, on the Isle of Mull, 1590.

"I'll keep us on course toward the sea-gate," Gripping the birlinn's rudder, Calum called to his brother.

Thunder boomed and lightning slashed the rippling waves of Duart Bay with a sizzling crackle, the fieriest welcome home Calum MacLean had ever received. Ahead on the inland rise, the thick stone walls of Duart Castle rose with forbidding height into the night sky.

"Look. Only one of our galleys remains anchored," Colin shouted as he lowered the sail.

"Aye, we'll make haste." Such a sight did not bode well with the depth of the current feud raging between the clans.

Their vessel skimmed the water as it cruised in, and his brother leaped into the waist-deep waves, seized the bow and roped it to a catch alongside the stone mooring.

The call of their arrival boomed from the tower guardsman.

Calum jumped onto the landing and jogged up the trail, Colin close behind him. The portcullis rose from within the stone-arched entrance gate, the clunky sound of its chains reverberating across the moors.

Arthur strode through in his thick fur boots. "Welcome home."

"Where's Lachlan?" Calum's chief had sent him to visit the Chief of MacLeod on Skye and Lachlan should be eager to hear his news.

"On the Isle of Islay. Lachlan received word Angus MacDonald had been captured by the king's men. Our chief didnae care to let this opportunity pass him by. Sixty of our warriors have gone with him. They intend to battle for the Rhinns."

Lachlan was determined to get his land on Islay's western coast back, and with Angus's capture, that would leave the MacDonald clan susceptible without their chief. A prime opportunity indeed, although not one he agreed with. 'Twas time for peace, though it seemed that would never come. "I bring news from my visit with MacLeod. Donald MacDonald too has been captured by the king. Donald and Angus both reside in Edinburgh's dungeons."

"'Tis a boon."

"When did Lachlan leave?"

"A few days past. I expect word soon. Did MacLeod agree to aid us?"

"Nay. With Donald's capture, he insisted there was no need." Lachlan's good fortune had doubled with both MacDonald chiefs in the king's hands. Lachlan would need to keep himself from discovery by the king's men too since they sought all three chiefs in this feud.

The heavens opened and the rain beat down.

"Come, we'll talk further inside." Calum strode into the great hall, Arthur at his side. "Colin and I will gather supplies and sail for Islay."

"That might no' be for the best." Arthur clasped his shoulder. "John MacIan has issued a call-to-arms."

Damn. It seemed every clan surrounding them wished a

fight. It'd been a year since John MacIan's release from Lachlan's dungeons, and if John wished to retaliate, now was the perfect time. As Lachlan's second, Calum would have to remain here in his chief's stead. "Aye, you're right."

"Brother, I can travel to Islay if you wish." Colin shook his dark head, splattering drops over the tapestry covered wall. "I'll ensure Lachlan does no' act too rashly."

"Nay, if MacIan is making his move, 'twould be best for you to travel to Tobermory and join the watchman there. Bring me word of any changes."

Colin wouldn't fail him, as he wouldn't fail Lachlan in his duty to protect their clan.

"Are ye Calum MacLean?" An old woman staggered to her feet from a wooden bench before the blazing hearth. She tapped her walking stick on the floor and jingled the multitude of silver bangles adorning her wrists.

"I am. Who are you?" He crossed and offered her a steadying hand.

"I've been waiting for ye. The past must be set to rights. A woman will come. Ye must keep her safe from the sea, and never let her go."

"What ramblings are these? Again, who are you?"

"Ye are the enemy, yet your heart is pure. She will aid ye, as ye will aid her." She pressed a brass charm into his hand. "Ye were but a lad when she left. I have another charm to gift her, and I shall see it done. Ye are both bound and must embrace your coming visions. Ye will have them because of her, until all things are set right. Allow them to guide ye." She tottered past Colin and Arthur and out the door.

Never had he had a more confusing conversation. The woman should take care she wasn't called out as a witch for her words of foretelling. 'Twas dangerous days for such. "Who is she, Arthur?"

"A fortuneteller, though she didnae admit such. She's been

waiting for your return and wouldnae speak of her concerns with any other."

He faced his brother. "Halt her. She cannae leave in this weather. At least offer her a pallet for the night. Tell her no harm shall come to her if she remains here."

Colin marched out the door.

The charm in his palm heated. *Ye were but a lad when she left.* He traced the inscription lit by the golden glow of the fire's flames.

Lila.
My charm.
Calum.

Lila. Her name resonated inside him. When he'd been just a lad, he'd been hunting in the forest with his father and seen a falling star. Grief had overwhelmed him, so swift and unexplainable.

Needing an answer for what he'd been told, he strode out the door.

Colin stood in the inner courtyard glancing in all directions. "Where is the woman?"

"Gone, Calum. She disappeared with nary a trace."

"'Tis impossible. She must be somewhere." He trotted up the stairs to the battlements and gripped the thick stone crenellation. Beyond, the moors were clear. No fortuneteller.

* * * *

For three nights, he'd been drawn to the eerie silence of the battlements, his soul restless and needy. This eve, the moon shimmered over the still loch, with not the slightest breeze to draw a ripple. The earth shook, and he clutched the charm he'd been unable to release.

Thrice this day the ground had moved so.

Possibly a bad omen. This morn, their warriors had returned

from Islay, though missing their chief and a score of men. Lachlan had been captured and taken to Edinburgh, and their casualties had been great.

Duart was now his to protect from the enemy's hands.

He wouldn't fail his chief, nor his clan.

Pressing the charm to his chest, he closed his eyes.

Solace came when he did.

Chapter 1

On the way to the ruins of Mingary Castle, the seat of the MacIans of Ardnamurchan, Scotland, 2014.

Riding a mountain bike, Lila MacIan negotiated the stony downward trail near Mingary Castle. Birds chirped from the odd pine tree clinging to the craggy hillside, and salty sea spray drifted in the breeze and tickled her nose. This was the way to enjoy nature at its very finest. "How much farther, Zayn?"

"We're close. Mingary's around the tip." Zayn MacKeane skidded his bike to a stop. Gravel thunked the rocks scattered along the grassy verge.

"Thank you for bringing me." She pulled in beside the energetic eighteen-year-old. The sound's blue-green waters glistened under the midday sun. The Isle of Mull, with its grassy moors and forested hills, appeared a lush jewel across the waterway. In times of old, Mull had been the land of her clan's enemy, though that could never take away from the isle's sheer beauty now. If only Nanna was here to see this with her, not missing somewhere in Scotland with the police and her endlessly searching.

"Are you okay?" Zayn nudged her shoulder. "You're

looking lost again."

"I'm fine." Or she would be, once she found her grandmother. "You make a wonderful tour guide. I'm so glad I stumbled across you at the museum and you agreed to bring me." Mingary had been on Nanna's travel itinerary. Where Nanna had intended to go, so would she.

"Stumbled is right." He grinned and rubbed his bruised calf. "You certainly know how to catch a person's attention."

"Sorry." She'd tripped over Zayn as he'd been searching under an exhibit display table with his long legs poking out.

"Since we're kin, you're forgiven." He shot her a mischievous grin.

"Yes, about that. How is it possible we're related? You never said." She'd shown her grandmother's picture to people in his village. So many MacIans, but none had seen Nanna.

"You're a MacIan, and I'm a MacKeane. Same pronunciation, just different letters. That happened a lot in the old days. People mixed up the spelling and it stuck."

"So you're saying we're from the same clan? John MacIan of Mingary's line?"

"Yep, though you have the strangest accent of any MacIan I know."

"In my opinion you're the one with the strange accent."

"So says the Aussie."

"And I'm proud to be one. Oi, oi, oi."

He chuckled. "Why is it Aussies say that?"

"You started it by saying Aussie. It's a chant we like to cheer at sports games, and wherever else takes our fancy. You say Aussie, and I say oi. Now no dissing my heritage or at least the non-Scots side."

"There's nothing to diss on the Scots side. We're a staunch clan and never say a word wrong."

"Now that's a little hard for me to disagree with." Goodness, Nanna would have loved to have met Zayn. He was so funny.

She dug into the pocket of her black Nike sports leggings and pulled out her brass charm. After Nanna had arrived in Scotland a month ago, she'd couriered this coin to her in Sydney. It had provided such comfort to have it close by. Rubbing its smooth disk-like surface, she picked up the trace of letters, an inscription which meant little, yet she adored it all the same.

Lila.
My charm.
Calum.

"That looks old. Can I take a look?" Zayn was the son of the museum's resident historian.

"Be careful with it." She handed it over. "My grandmother received this from a fortuneteller at Edinburgh's markets, or at least that's what she said in her note. It's a MacIan relic from the 1500s. Obviously I'm not the Lila that's mentioned, but it's lovely it holds my name all the same. I didn't even know Lila was Scots in origin."

"I've got a cousin called Lilias. We call her Lila for short. This could be a shortened version too." He smoothed over the etching. "These charms are often referred to as coins or tokens, and this one's in mint condition. You should show my dad. He might know more considering it's inscribed. Did your grandmother tell you anything about it when she gifted it to you?"

"Not much. She said to keep it on me at all times, and to never let it go, which I've done. What do you think about the etching? It sounds kind of romantic to me, like Lila is Calum's charm."

"Hmm, it could be that the piece holds a double meaning. Maybe Calum gifted this charm to Lila?" He handed the coin back. "I'm sorry none of us have seen your grandmother."

"I'm going to find her." She'd never give up her search, no matter where or how long it took her. Tears came to her eyes and she forced them back as she pocketed the precious coin. "Did you remember to bring your wetsuit?"

"Sure did. I've got my snorkeling gear too." He patted his black and blue checked backpack strapped over his shoulders. "Even though it's autumn, I've been known to take a dip right up until Christmas Day. I'm game for a swim if you are."

"When I was wandering about the museum's displays, I read about a storm driving a Spanish Armada ship into the sound. It was a few centuries ago, but it capsized right here at the tip of Ardnamurchan. Apparently a treasure trove of gold coins has never been found."

"I know the story, but I doubt we'll find the bounty. No one ever has."

"I'd love one of those coins." It could finance a broader search for Nanna. The police were doing what they could, but a woman couldn't disappear without a trace. No. She had to do everything she could to find—

The ground shook. Nesting birds cackled and took flight from the trees. They swept down the ridge and along the track in front of her. Feet planted either side of her bike, she waited until the shaking eased. "Does that happen often?"

"We rarely get earthquakes." He thrust his foot into the pedal. "Let's get off this hill."

"Good idea." Loose rocks could easily dislodge and tumble down. She shoved her white shirtsleeves to her elbows.

"Mingary awaits. How about a race?" Grinning, Zayn took off.

"Hey, you cheat. Wait up." Flying downhill, she rode hard in pursuit. Ahead, Mingary's ruins perched on a massive ridge of rock overlooking the sea. The castle's thick walls stood three stories high and exactly as her grandmother had described in her tales. Nanna had spent time here in her younger years and adored this place.

Zayn slowed. "Are you up for a little bit of history on the homeward straight?"

"Absolutely." She'd absorbed what she could at the museum, but Zayn had lived here all his life. He'd be a treasure trove of information.

"John MacIan was the last MacIan to hold Mingary before the Campbell of Argyll took possession."

"I read about that in the archives. MacIan lost his first wife in childbirth, and when he could have wed a woman young enough to bear him children in his later years, he instead married Janet Campbell, his enemy's mother from Mull."

"Yes. Supposedly to bring some calm to the feud that raged through these isles at the time, and usually those kinds of alliances saw success, but in this case it didn't. At the time Lachlan MacLean was the chief across the way, and he was a warrior well known for using any unlawful means to achieve what he wanted. Dad's always talking about that time in history. It's one of his favorite eras."

"I should have brought the book I picked up about the MacIan clan with me. It covered that period. Your father recommended it, but I left it in my hotel room." The wind whipped her hair across her face.

"Watch the dip. It's a bit rough here, Lila."

"Thanks." She lifted off her seat and missed the jarring impact of the bump. "They need to fix this trail."

"The constant rain messes with it, but from here on to Mingary it evens out."

They rode along the final lowland stretch to the bluff.

"We have nothing like this back home. I mean castles and all."

"I've always wanted to visit Australia. Does it feel like you're walking around on your head down there?"

"No." She laughed, something she hadn't done since the

day Nanna had gone missing. "I wish Nanna was here. She'd like you."

"Have you got any other family?"

"It's just me and her." The castle loomed. She pulled to a stop alongside the entrance and propped her bike against the stone wall. The castle's land-gate appeared no more than a darkened doorway leading into its gloomy recesses. "I was expecting a gatehouse and all the trappings. Where is it all?"

"It used to have gate and a drawbridge, but they were lost over time." Zayn butted his bike against hers. "This entrance leads straight into the inner courtyard. Let me show you around."

"Do you come here a lot? It's so close to the village." She crept inside then swept away the cobwebs stretching the width of stone passageway.

"I lived here most of last summer. Dad's on the finance team for Mingary's restoration, and we began the cleanup back then."

"What cleanup?" Moss grew in clumps along sections of the walls. Keeping clear of the muddy rubble littering the path, she jumped from stone to stone. "Sorry, that was rude. You've clearly done a bang-up job. The place looks nice and cozy." She barely hid her grin.

"Funny, but I meant outside. No one's allowed to touch the inside until the experienced crew arrives."

"I see." She rounded the corner, and the sun shone down into Mingary's inner courtyard. The surrounding curtain walls, several feet thick, gave evidence of the castle's initial strength and how it had managed to stand strong for so long. A shame it had been left to go to ruin. "This place must have looked incredible in its heyday. In one museum display, it showed this place had pinkish-white stones."

"They lost their color over time. Plain old gray now."

"Though so much is still intact." She wandered around the open base of a well flooded with water and spilling its excess over the stone floor.

"Careful. Fairly intact, but slippery."

"I'll be—" Her vision hazed, and she grasped the wall. An image materialized in her mind, showing the well's sides rising to waist height with ivy trailing over them. Someone stood next to it in a beautiful olive gown, but as she tried to focus, the image shimmered away.

"Are you okay?"

"Yes, my imagination is playing tricks with me." She was seeing things she shouldn't and it was likely stress. She hadn't exactly been sleeping well since Nanna's disappearance. "Is there anything else I need to watch out for?"

Zayn motioned toward the seaside wall. "There's a small patch there in danger of collapse, but since that tremor we had earlier didn't knock it over, I'm sure we'll be fine."

"It'll be great when this place is returned to its former glory. When will the restoration crew arrive?"

"After the winter." He swung his backpack off. "We should take that swim while the sun is high and leave exploring the castle until later. There's an area outside near the sea-gate entrance where we can change."

"That sounds perfect." She followed him out, collected her gear from the back of her bike then climbed down the steep trail toward the rocky beach. On the loch side, Mingary perched imposingly high on the forty foot rock wall above. Back in the day, the guardsmen patrolling the battlements would have had a bird's eye view across the sound. A prime position.

"Over here, Lila." Zayn waved her toward the rocks.

She sat on a squat stone, lugged her wetsuit, flippers and mask out, then palmed her charm. *Soldier on, my dear. Never give up the fight.* Nanna's voice, words she'd impressed upon her since she was a child, kept her strong. She'd never give up. She'd find Nanna no matter where she was.

"You're holding onto that talisman like a lifeline." Zayn

eased onto the rock next to hers.

"It's the last thing Nanna gave me."

"I'm sorry. I lost one of my grandparents last year. It's not easy."

"She's not dead, just missing." She shoved more of those unwanted tears away and found her inner strength. "I'm sorry you've lost someone close to you."

"Death is so fast. I miss my grandpa. Dad's always got his nose stuck in a museum book, but Grandpa loved the outdoors as I do. At least once a month we fished and tramped together. Those times are long gone now." He stared out over the loch and slowly sighed.

Memories haunted her as well.

"Nanna's always spoken so fondly of this place. She lived here at Ardnamurchan when she was younger and she longed to return one day."

"When did she go missing?"

"A month ago. During her first week in Scotland, she toured Edinburgh Castle, rode the scenic city bus and visited the markets."

"What have the police said?"

"The last person to see her alive was the owner of the bed-and-breakfast where she stayed. The lady told the police Nanna didn't come down in the morning for breakfast, and when she went up to wake her, she was gone. Nanna's belongings still lay around her room, but there was no sign of her. She just disappeared."

"I'm glad you're looking for her."

"I don't know what else to do. I stayed in Edinburgh for a couple of weeks then made my way here. This seemed the next logical place to—" The ground shook again and she clutched the rock underneath her. "That's two earthquakes in such a short time. Do you think it'll be safe to swim?"

"The loch's only a mile or so wide. I doubt a tsunami is

possible. I'm game if you are."

"A swim would be good. Let's find some treasure so I have a ton of money to finance a massive search for my grandmother. The police are doing their thing, but so must I."

"Great. You can change over by the sea-gate wall. It curves around, giving plenty of privacy on the other side." He pulled his white t-shirt over his head and nodded toward the area. "And no peeking at me while you do."

"I promise." She ducked around the corner with her wetsuit, tugged it on and slipped her charm inside her zippered pocket. Her heart ached. She needed her grandmother back. "I miss you Nanna. From the depths of my soul, I wish I could find you, alive and well. I hate that we're apart."

The wind lifted her hair and made it tickle her face. Wishes. What she wouldn't give to have that one answered.

"Are you ready, Lila?"

"Coming." Mask and flippers in hand, she strode toward the shore where Zayn waited on the wet sand. "We're after sparkly and pretty, Zayn."

"Yeah, and plenty of it." He shuffled backward through the surf in his flippers.

She joined him, and at waist depth, popped her tube into her mouth, eased onto her belly and kicked out. Colorful fish darted all around as she swam toward a boulder with its slick rounded top breaking the water's surface. These rocks were everywhere. Hands planted on top, she hauled herself up and sat on the peak. The incoming tide lapped her back.

Zayn tugged his mask down around his neck as he bobbed in the water. "Look behind you. We've got company."

A slick-skinned dolphin grazed the rough stone as the creature rounded it. "Maybe she wants to play."

"There's more than one." Zayn shoved his mask back on and swam toward a second dolphin. "The waters teem with seals too, so keep an eye out. They're not as friendly as the dolphins."

"Thanks for the warning." The dolphin nearest her let out a chorus of squeals then circled the rock she sat on.

"I'm going to try to catch a ride." Zayn grasped his dolphin's fin, and it pulled him out of the water and took off. He let out a loud whoop.

She laughed then stopped as the boulder shook. A wave tumbled her into the water. The current dragged her down and everything blackened.

Fighting to hold onto her breath, she clawed for the surface.

Stars blazed all around, a multitude so bright she slammed her eyes shut. The water sucked her deeper. She had to get out.

An arm clamped around her waist.

She jerked around. A man with piercing golden eyes tightened his hold on her and pointed upward. Yes, upward. That's where she had to go, now.

He pushed them through the murky depths and in a fizz of bubbles, they broke the surface.

She pulled her mask off and gulped in air. "I love you. Where did you come from?"

"Love already, lass? The lights blazed and I dove in." Dark hair was plastered to his face and neck as he treaded water. "Can you swim? The shore is close."

"Yes, but where's Zayn?"

"There's another out here with you?" He searched the water.

"Zayn took a dolphin ride. Hopefully he didn't get caught by the rogue wave like I did. It pulled me under so fast. Goodness, its dark." Afternoon had turned to evening. "How is it so late?" Dizziness overwhelmed her and she grabbed her head.

"I cannae see another. 'Tis only us." His Scots brogue was thicker than Zayn's, his words far harder to understand. Although that could be the head spinning too. She needed rest, or to catch a decent breath.

"He must be okay." He hadn't been near her when the wave

hit. "Please, who do I have to thank for saving my life?"

"Calum MacLean." The waves bumped them together.

"There was an earthquake. I should've taken more care."

"Aye, there've been unusual happenings this day. Thrice the earth moved."

Thrice? Who said thrice anymore?

Behind her, a small island jutted off shore and around it, the waters branched off in three different directions. This wasn't Mingary's beach. "Ah, where am I?"

"Duart Castle on Mull."

Miles from where she should have been. No wonder Zayn wasn't here. "Really?"

"Aye, let's get you to land."

Yes. She'd figure things out once her feet were back on solid ground. She tried to kick, but her limbs shook.

"I've got you, lass." His hold was tight as he cut a fast path through the churning waters, his strength alone propelling them forward. At hip depth, he stood and with his arm around her waist, helped her onto the beach. Frowning, he eyed her. "What is this you're wearing? It looks like sealskin and 'tis equally as dark. I've no' seen such cloth afore."

"It's a wetsuit."

"Has this come from the continents?"

More of his strange speech, and the Western Isles weren't exactly in the backwaters.

"You can buy a wetsuit almost anywhere." She flopped onto her back on the sand. The moon hovered on the horizon, casting a golden wash over the castle's massive stone walls. Duart stood high on the rise of a craggy hill a few hundred feet inland, its fortified walls topped with battlements and tower house windows lit with candlelight. "Zayn will be terribly worried."

"Is he your next of kin?" Calum knelt over her, pressed callused palms against her cheeks. "I'll ensure he's informed you've been found safe and well."

"My grandmother's my next of kin, but Zayn needs to know."

"What village do you hail from?"

"Sydney, though it's hardly a village."

"Are you no' from Mull?" He flattened his palm against her forehead. "Your skin is cold."

"This is my first trip to Scotland, and it appears I took an unexpected detour to your isle at that. And the wetsuit is keeping me warm where it counts." She edged up on her elbows. Along the barbican, guardsmen patrolled the two-story gatehouse. In great plaids no less. She'd read Duart was a fully functioning castle and open to tourists, but this sight was truly amazing. He must be one of the staff. "Do you work here?"

"This is my home."

"You sure keep things realistic for the visitors."

"Lass, your words are odd. I dinnae understand why you speak so." He stared into her eyes. "Aye, and you have the same silver eyes as Mistress Jean who arrived a month past. She too had a strange accent, more like the Lowlanders. What is your name?"

"Lila." She had Nanna's uniquely colored eyes, and he'd said Jean, her grandmother's name. Fingers numb, she clutched his soggy shirtfront. "Tell me what Mistress Jean looks like."

"You're Lila?" Eyebrows soaring, he slid his hands over hers.

"Yes. What does Mistress Jean look like?"

"Elderly. Black hair with a touch of gray. She wore unusual clothing the eve she arrived. What she called pa-ja-mas." He twisted his tongue around the word, as if finding it foreign. "I was in the chief's solar when Lachlan questioned her. She was found wandering this beach, lost and confused."

The hair color was right, and the pajamas were a good sign. Nanna had disappeared during the night after she'd gone to bed, but that had been in Edinburgh, not this far across the country. "What was her last name?"

"Cunningham. After discovering she'd arrived on Mull, she spent some time with the chief's wife. Margaret too was a Cunningham afore she wed and they enjoyed each other's company. She was no' here long, mayhap a sennight afore she continued on."

"To where?" Even though their last name was MacIan, Nanna's maiden name had been Cunningham. It could well be her.

"No' a soul saw her leave. She vanished into the night just as she'd come."

Yes, the timing was perfect, never mind the location. She couldn't let this information slip by without being fully checked over.

"I need to make a call. The person you've described sounds like my grandmother, and she's been missing for the same length of time." Excited, she tugged her flippers off, grabbed his wide shoulders and hauled herself up. Oh, he was hot, hard, and heavily muscled. At his wrist a sheathed dagger glinted, and lower still, his leather pants clung to his powerful thighs. Definitely authentic. She wobbled on shaky legs. "Nice warrior attire."

Frowning, he offered her a hand. "Does your head feel clear? You were under the water for some time."

"My head is—" Her thoughts swirled, and an image flickered through her mind. She grasped hold of the vision.

This man walked beside her across the moors. The late afternoon sunshine bathed his tanned forearms as he opened his hand and stroked a brass coin. "This is mine, so I may keep you close," he said.

"Can I hold it?" she asked him. "Only for a bit."

"Nay, you have your own, and this one I need to keep you close." He glanced ahead at a fallen log barring the trail, scooped her into his arms and carried her over it.

"Calum, you're very good at keeping me close, whether you hold that charm or not." She breathed in the fresh air, picking up an alluring scent. "Where are you taking me?"

"To a place of great beauty." He set her back on her feet at the top of the rise. Spread out in the meadow below, a wash of yellow and red wildflowers swayed in the gentle breeze.

"This is beautiful."

"Aye, though this was a place of great sadness so few years ago."

"What happened to cause that?"

"A great battle. Many of our warriors perished in this field, but now the wildflowers remind all who walk here that our lost kin still live, even though no' among us."

She rubbed her cheek against his shoulder. "You have a soft heart."

"Nay, I am a warrior."

"That too, but your heart's a gooey mess and it's all mine."

"Lila." He growled her name. "You must take care with your strange words. We spoke about this."

"Yes, you spoke and I decided not to listen. Nothing unusual there, and by now, you should be used to it." She grinned, and the sweet fragrance in the air teased more memories to stir. "Nanna used to take me to the markets every Monday morning to buy hoards of fresh stock for the shop she managed. I love flowers, particularly roses."

He kissed the tip of her nose. "As I—"

"Lila?" Calum gripped her arms. "You appear in a daze."

"Sorry, my imagination keeps getting away on me today." Never in her twenty-one years had she experienced a doozy of a vision like that one. She didn't even know this man, yet had recalled a conversation with him as if it were real.

"We must speak." His golden gaze flickered with determination. "I was drawn outside to the loch this eve, as I have the past three nights since I returned from Skye. A fortuneteller told me a woman would come. That I should aid you, and keep you safe from the sea."

"What?" If he truly wished to aid her, all she needed was the use of a phone. She shook the sand from her flippers. "I need to call the authorities. You don't mind telling them about seeing my grandmother, do you?"

"Since my chief's capture, I'm the only authority on this isle. Come." He strode toward the sand dunes, fetched a sword tossed atop a plaid and belted it over his hips. It glinted razor sharp in the moonlight.

"Knowing Nanna might have come through here after her disappearance is the best news. I have to make that call then be on my way."

"'Tis too late to be making calls, and 'tis now my duty to see to your welfare."

"But the police are available twenty-four hours a day." Well, they were in Australia. Surely that was the same in Scotland.

"Again, come. We'll speak inside."

Yes, they would speak.

He'd seen her grandmother and she had to get to the bottom of this.

The way she'd arrived and these visions she'd experienced weren't right.

She needed to sort this. Now.

Chapter 2

Calum flapped the sand from his plaid and wrapped it gently around Lila's shoulders. The so-called wetsuit she wore molded every curve of her body, and 'twas best none of his men caught sight of it. She snuggled into his tartan, and with a hand at her back, he led her up the grassy rise and into the keep. He signaled the guard to lower the portcullis for the night. Lila was here, and deep within him, he knew her, even though they'd never met before. The fortuneteller had said they were bound, and to embrace his coming visions. He would have them because of her, until all things were set right.

"This place is amazing." Her gaze roamed in all directions. "You said before your chief had been captured. What did you mean by that?"

"Three days past, during a recent battle on the Isle of Islay, Lachlan was caught by clan MacDonald then handed over to the king's men. The dungeons will be where he'll remain while the king has his way."

"The king still has dungeons?" She scratched her head. "Oh, I get it. Authenticity. I realize you live here, but you don't have to keep the act going for me."

"There is no act. Duart is mine to protect with Lachlan's

son still so young.”

“Seriously, take a break.” She smiled and wagged a finger at him. “Opening hours must be over by now.”

More of her strange words.

“This way.” He bypassed the great hall where his clan would be enjoying their evening meal and instead escorted Lila up the tower’s side stairs and into his chamber. He closed the door, crossed the room and stoked the fire to blazing life. “I’ll have you warm soon.” He added another log.

“This is amazing.” She wandered to his side table, set her flippers down then picked up the pitcher and poured water into the basin. “What a beautiful antique.” She traced along the rim.

“’Twas gifted to me, but ’tis no antique.”

“Oh, sorry. It looks like one.” She drifted to his desk, inspected his candleholder then glanced at the ceiling. “Now that’s strange. The wall sconces in the hallway were lit by candlelight, but how come there aren’t any lights or electricity? I heard Duart had gone through several restorations.”

“What are you speaking about, lass? Do you feel well?”

“Yes, but I’m anxious.” Her silver eyes sparkled, the most magical color. “I really can’t wait until the morning to make that call.” She nibbled on her lush lower lip. “Zayn lives in Kilchoan. I have his number.”

“What number do you speak of?” Ardnamurchan was the enemy’s land.

“Ah, that would be number you dial”—she lifted a brow—“when using a phone.”

Aye, she was no’ yet of sound mind after her adventurous dip in the loch. He tucked a drying strand of black hair behind her ear, his fingers brushing her earlobe. Tingles raced along his fingertips. “I’ll call a healer in the morn if your head has still no’ cleared.”

“My head is fine, and you’ve really got to stop acting like this is the sixteenth century. I’d enjoy it if I were a tourist, but not right now. I have people to call."

"'Tis the sixteenth century. The year of our Lord, fifteen-ninety." The fortuneteller had said 'twas his duty to aid her. Whether she was confused or not, he would. "What year do you believe it is?"

"Not believe. It's twenty-fourteen." She glanced around his chamber. "You're clearly letting your work get to you. You have a quill, but no pen. You have candles, and no light bulbs. You have a trunk, yet no dresser. You're wearing warrior attire and have a sword. You have no phone, and you've never heard of a wetsuit or Sydney. But in the real world, those things exist."

"Mayhap you'd rather I call a healer now?"

"Grrreat. Let's do that." She sank onto the end of his bed and fisted his brown fur covers. "Maybe the healer will allow me to borrow his phone and call Zayn, unless you're all in on this act together."

The fortuneteller had never said the woman would have such—his vision clouded and he grasped the wooden desk chair. He envisioned Lila sitting on his bed, speaking to him. She tugged the tight sleeve of her wetsuit up and uncovered a well-crafted piece of metal strapped to her wrist. She angled it toward him then pressed a knob on the side. It lit as if sunlight was contained within.

He blinked and the image melted away.

Aye, the visions had begun as the fortuneteller had said.

On his knees, he gripped her cold hands. "Show me the contraption you have on your wrist."

"How did you—never mind. Of course I'll show you if it'll help you accept what I've been saying." She lowered the plaid he'd wrapped around her then showed him the piece. "This is a watch, and don't tell me you haven't seen one of these before."

"'Tis impressive. In my vision, you lit it up."

"You've had a vision too? I've had them as well today."

"What did you see? I was told they'd come."

"The last one was of us wandering through a meadow. You spoke of warriors dying there. Is there a field somewhere here with an abundance of wildflowers?"

"There is. Did your vision show you this?"

"Yes." She clasped shaky hands in her lap. "Who told you these visions would come?"

"An old woman. Show me the light."

She pressed the device's side and light flared. "This watch has a battery which conveys electricity."

"'Tis a magical device." Incredible. He crossed the room, gathered her flippers from the side table and shook the webbed ends. "These appear as if they would aid you in moving swiftly through the water, as duck's feet would."

"Yes, they do. Take a look at my mask as well." She slid it from around her neck and handed it over.

He pressed it against his face as he'd first seen it on her. Rimming his eyes and nose, it stuck to his skin.

"The tube on the side goes into your mouth and allows you to swim without the need to come up for air." She stood behind him and angled it just so.

"'Tis clever." Aye, her belongings were wondrous, and she'd come to him from the sea, amongst a burst of enthralling lights. He cupped her cheek, stroked his thumb across her smooth skin. "'Tis my duty to aid you, and the past must be set to rights, yet you speak of coming from the future. Certainly you have strange belongings which dinnae exist, but I've no' spoken a mistruth. The year is fifteen-ninety. Do you too speak the truth?" Anything was possible considering the old woman's words.

"Yes." She paced the chamber. "If what we're both saying is true, then that means I've traveled through time, which would explain a few things."

"If you've come from the future, then 'tis a miracle. I was told you'd come, by a fortuneteller who gave me a charm."

"A fortuneteller gave Nanna a charm too. Oh, this is crazy. Incredible, but crazy." She dug into her pocket, pulled out a coin and passed it across. "Nanna sent me this charm, along with a note telling me to never let it go. Are you the Calum mentioned on this coin? It's a relic from this time."

Carefully, he smoothed over the inscription. "Aye. My coin is identical to yours." He fished it from his pocket and passed it to her. "Three days past, a fortuneteller gave this to me. She said the past must be set to rights. That you would come, and that I must keep you safe from the sea and never let you go. She said we are bound, and to embrace the coming visions."

"I can't believe I've traveled through time." She stared at it. "Yet it all makes eerie sense. How else could I have ended up here, miles from where I should have been?"

"Gifted charms are considered lucky talismans. Ours appear to hold some kind of magical power too."

"Nanna's here as well, in the past." She bent, hands to her knees as she sucked in a long breath. "I made a wish upon my charm, not long before I tumbled into the water and was dragged under. I asked to find Nanna, alive and well. She went missing from the future, and now I finally know where she disappeared to. I have to find her."

"We shall, as soon as it is safe to do so. War rages, and far too close to our shores." He tipped up her chin and traced along her lower lip. "It appears charms and wishes have brought you to me. You understand you cannae speak of this? Claims of such would be considered witchery and lead you no' to your grandmother, but the stake."

"I understand." She rested her forehead against his chest then wrapped her shaky hands around his waist. "Sorry, a little shock is setting in."

"We're bound by these charms and by a fortuneteller's decree." He pulled her closer. "I willnae fail in my duty to you."

"Thank you, and regardless of whatever magic brought me

here, I'm glad it was to you."

"As am I."

Relief coursed through him.

She was his, and she was back.

* * * *

Lila snuggled into Calum's embrace. She'd made a wish and something magical had happened, except she'd arrived at a time of great feuding between her clan and Calum's. Nanna had also told those here she was a Cunningham and not a MacIan, a wise move. Doing so would give Nanna the protection of another clan's name, a clan who weren't deeply immersed in this particular war. A precaution she needed to take too.

A wave of emotions tumbled through her, shock and fear, as well as apprehension over what lay ahead, and relief at being so much closer to finding Nanna. Overcome, she shuddered and tangled her fingers in his damp shirt.

"Are you all right?" Calum stroked her back, his touch warm and firm.

"I wished for this. I'll be fine once I've had some time to take it all in." And once she'd armed herself with as much information as she could. "Does John MacIan hold Mingary?"

"Aye, and the MacIans and MacDonalds are at war against my kin."

"Can you tell me about it?"

"The feud has raged for years. Lachlan MacLean, along with Donald and Angus MacDonald each received a missive from the king requesting they present themselves at court to atone for their actions. The king wished a discussion with all three chiefs, but Lachlan had no intention of traveling to Edinburgh. That choice is now out of his hands. He was captured during a battle with the MacDonalds on Islay. 'Twas a grave fight that took many of my men's lives."

"What of the other two chiefs?"

"Donald and Angus were captured afore that battle. With all

three chiefs now at the king's mercy, it appears those discussions will occur whether Lachlan wished them to or no'."

"I'm sorry." She couldn't have arrived at a more difficult time. "You mentioned Margaret before, that the chief's wife spent time with Nanna. Can I speak to her?"

"In the morn. She'll be tending her bairns this eve." He released her and crossed to his trunk. He snagged a white tunic and passed it across. "A nightrail, or as close as I can offer."

Yes, she'd stay the night, and however long her wish kept her here in the past.

"I'll leave so you may change."

"No, don't go." She clutched his arm. "Stay, but turn your back. Please, I don't want to be left alone."

"Aye, mayhap 'tis for the best. I've no wish to leave you either." He turned and the longer strands of his dark hair brushed his shoulders.

"Thank you." She laid her charm on his nightstand then wriggled out of the clingy wetsuit and pulled his tunic over her head. "Where should I sleep?"

"My bed. I'll sleep afore the fire."

"Are you certain?"

"Take my bed, lass."

"Okay, but if you want it back, just yell out." She scrambled across his huge bed and dived under the covers. Near the fire, he tugged his damp shirt off and slung it across the corner wooden chair. His chest held a smattering of hair, the same dark shade as his head, and his arms and shoulders were packed with muscle. Contoured abs rippled as he dipped a cloth in the water basin and wiped it over his glorious golden skin. A thrill chased through her. Clearly a warrior who fought by the sword, and a wonderful distraction from her turbulent thoughts.

"Another vision." He seized the edge of the table and closed his eyes.

"Are you all right?"

"Aye." Slowly he straightened and smiled. "Interesting. You, my charm, have a beautiful heart shaped mole on your belly."

"What? Do you care to explain?"

"In my vision, I saw you lying afore me in a darkened cave."

"And I somehow pulled up my shirt and you caught sight of my belly?"

"There was no shirt, though you were otherwise covered with my plaid."

"I've never shown anyone that mole, and exactly what do you mean by otherwise covered?"

"'Tis best I leave it at that." He removed his sword belt, loosened the ties of his leather pants and gripped the waistband.

"Wait." She slammed her eyes shut. "Make sure you put on lots of clothing, layers and layers of it. No matter what you've seen, we are still setting some boundaries." And what were these visions all about? She'd never had them until today.

"I prefer to sleep as I was born."

"And I prefer you don't. Just keep your pants on mister."

"Move over, Lila." His voice was husky and far too close. "We sleep together."

She shoved her eyes open. He towered over her, but thankfully, he'd donned a new pair of soft cotton pants. "You said you'd sleep before the fire."

"I've changed my mind."

"Because of that vision?"

"I need to remain close to you. The urge to do so is strong." He slid in beside her. "Your arrival was foretold, and these visions prove we shall be close."

"No, they prove we're seeing visions." Except a niggle told her he was right. She wriggled over to make room for him. "I can handle sharing a bed, but no more heart shaped mole peek-shows for you." She yanked the covers up to her nose, and his fresh outdoor scent trapped within the cotton drifted around her. He smelt sooo good, like the wind and sea, an intoxicating mix. "And stay on your side of the bed."

"Both sides are mine."

"They aren't tonight." Did that mean he was single? He certainly better be or else he could get back out again. "You don't have a woman somewhere, do you?"

"Nay." One firm word. "It appears there is only you."

A hundred butterflies abounded in her belly. "That's a nice one-liner."

"I need to hold you. I've no desire for distance."

"I'm here for Nanna. I made a wish to find her, not end up in bed with you."

"Tell me about your grandmother." He rolled toward her, wrapped an arm around her waist. She should pull away, only she couldn't.

"She's the most amazing person and raised me singlehandedly. When I was five and old enough to understand that most children had parents, Nanna took me to a memorial statue near the ocean where one can lay flowers for those lost at sea. I crawled onto Nanna's lap and she told me all about my father. John had been a great man, one who'd led others, but he'd sailed on a vessel that had been caught and gone down in a storm. Nanna said she was without any images of him, but she took her notebook out of her purse and drew a picture for me. She sat him on a horse with a sword in his hand." That memory filled her heart and made her smile. "Nanna's always been into all things historical. She even sketched my mother standing next to him in a long-flowing gown with flowers braided in her hair. It was the prettiest picture and I kept it pinned to the wall above my bed."

"Was your mother with him? Was she too lost at sea?"

"No, she died giving birth to me. I arrived very early and well, she died. Nothing could be done. She battled though, for two days through labor.”

“You said at the loch you had no other kin?”

“Yes, though Nanna decided to return to Scotland so she could try to find family, even if remote. It’s been twenty-one years since she was last here. We were even going to meet up and travel the Highlands together just a week after she went missing. I couldn’t come straight away because of work.” A job she’d been given extended leave from since she hadn’t a clue how long the search would take. “What about your kin? Have you always lived here?”

“Aye, my father was a warrior as I am, and my mother a seamstress. Eight years ago during my twentieth winter, a deadly sickness of the lungs took the lives of many on Mull. They both perished, along with thirty others.”

“Do you have anyone else?”

“My brother is away but should return soon. I also have an entire clan. I’ve never been without kin.” He played with her hair, winding it around his fingers. Her scalp tingled in the most delicious way.

“I sure would have loved a sibling.” She wriggled closer and rubbed her nose against his warm skin, right over his heart where the beat pounded strong. “The strangest thoughts are going through my mind.”

“Aye, ’tis the same for me. We are bound, as the fortuneteller foretold.”

Yes, never in her life had she been this relaxed with a man. “So, do you have any interesting moles yourself?”

“Nay, but I do possess a curious looking birthmark on my right cheek.” He smoothed down her side, over her hip and cupped the curve of her bottom. “Right about here.”

“You’re getting rather touchy-feely.”

“So are you.”

Because she couldn’t damn well help it. She tip-toed her fingers down his bare chest. Ties partly unfastened, his pants sat low on his hips. "What's your birthmark look like?"

"Take a guess." One sly grin. "Or would you care to see it?"

"I would say yes, but maybe another time, when I've known you for longer than a few short hours."

"A sound idea." He dropped a kiss on the top of her head. "Tell me more about this place you call home."

"I live on the other side of the world, in a country as yet undiscovered. Sydney is a bustling city where buildings are far taller than this castle and they stand row upon row." But she'd rather learn more about him. "What's it like living here?"

"'Tis my home and I would live nowhere else."

"It must be nice to have a home." Without Nanna, she now had none. Their small apartment certainly hadn't provided her any solace since Nanna's awful disappearance. She lifted up onto her elbows. On the bedside table, firelight flickered over her talisman and lit the inscription. "Is it possible to find the fortuneteller who gave you your charm? Since they're identical, she must have been the one to give Nanna mine. She may be able to impart more knowledge."

"She vanished mere moments after handing it to me. Although she spoke of having another charm to gift, and she'd see it done." He stroked her cheek and stared into her eyes. "You're now in my care, and I gladly offer you my protection. You will always be safe with me."

"I know." Deep inside her, that knowledge rang with truth. Except he was still a MacLean, her enemy. Nanna had used the last name of Cunningham, as she would too. Until she learnt more, she'd take every precaution.

"'Tis been a long day. You should rest." He settled her back against him and tucked her head under his chin. "I'll watch over you."

She closed her eyes and drifted, so content within his arms.

"Goodnight, Calum."

"Aye, 'tis a good night, my charm."

Chapter 3

Sunlight slivered through the wooden shutters over Calum's narrow window and woke him too soon. Lila slept in his arms, her heart beating against his and bringing such peace to his soul. Charms and wishes had brought them together, but they were bound by far more. She was his.

"Calum?" Rubbing her feet against his legs, she mumbled his name. "Is it morning already?"

"Shh, there's no need to awaken." If he could, he would hold her all day.

"There is when I have to find Nanna." She wriggled until she escaped him then arms raised, stretched and let out a contented sigh. "Mmm, I love the mornings. They're my favorite time of the day. So many possibilities lie ahead. Don't you think?" Her cheeks were rosy and pink, and the sprinkle of freckles across her nose made his fingers itch to trace them.

"I prefer the nights when my duties are done and I can rest, as I did last eve."

"Have you had any more visions of things to come?"

"Nay, and you?"

"Nope. I even had an undisturbed sleep, which hasn't happened since Nanna disappeared." She tweaked his nose.

"You don't snore either. A bonus."

"You'll need to take care how you speak. There are many who will question your strange words."

A rap sounded on the door. "Calum, 'tis Colin."

Good. His brother had returned from Tobermory. "I'll meet you in the chief's solar. I willnae be long," he called out. He shoved his bedcovers aside, strode to his trunk and dragged on a tunic.

"Who's Colin?" Lila crawled out of the covers and hopped off the end of his bed.

"My brother, the one I spoke of last eve." He nabbed his plaid, wrapped it around him then secured it with a silver pin across his chest.

"Can I meet him? Where's he been?"

"On watch along the coast."

"Watching whom?"

"John MacIan of Mingary. He's our greatest threat. Following John's marriage to Lachlan's mother, my chief tossed him into our dungeons. Lachlan believed John could be swayed to our side with the alliance, but his support toward his MacDonald kin remained unwavering."

"I read about John MacIan's nuptials with Janet Campbell." A wary expression crossed her face and she eased back a step. "Please tell me you didn't have anything to do with slaughtering MacIan's people on his wedding night."

That black night, Lachlan had attacked without warning, moving swiftly from chamber to chamber. He'd murdered MacIan's attendants where they'd slept, and when Janet's screams had pierced the night, Calum had jerked awake and flown from his bed. "I was too late."

"What do you mean?"

"When I arrived at Janet's chamber, Lachlan stood over MacIan, ready to slay him where he lay. Janet begged Lachlan for leniency, but he wouldnae listen. 'Twas fortunate Colin arrived moments after I did. It took both of us to subdue him."

"Your chief butchered eighteen people and all because he didn't get the alliance he wished for?" She shivered and rubbed her arms. "I wouldn't blame John MacIan if he desired retribution. How could you condone such an action?"

"I didnae condone it, but I gave my chief my oath. Virtue mine honor. I am loyal to him and my clan." She clearly didn't understand clan loyalty, and now wasn't the time to explain.

"Then perhaps the king is the only authority on this land who can adequately bring about justice. He has a far greater force, an entire army at his disposal compared to those of the clan chiefs."

"Highlanders fight for what is theirs, and the king shouldnae be permitted to rule over all of Scotland." Though there was also truth in what she said. Times were changing, and the clans would eventually have to move with that shift. Needing to hold her before he left, he backed her against the wall and planted his hands either side of her on the cold stone. "You may no' agree with my actions, but there's naught I can do. MacIan was released within the year, and now we await his vengeance."

"That's a terrible way to live, to always be at war. I can see I'll need to take great care while I'm here, but I can and will look after myself. Where I come from, women do."

"My oath to you stands firm. You have my protection and my aid."

"Thank you, but I'm strong in my own right." She ducked under his arm and walked to the window. With each step she took, his shirt molded itself sweetly to her bottom.

His cock hardened and made him wish for what he'd seen in his vision from the cave. She'd lain before him, a plaid pooled around her hips as he'd traced her beautiful mole with one finger. "I'll send a maid to you."

"I'd appreciate that."

'Twas best he leave before he no longer could. Quietly, he

closed the door behind him and trod down the passageway. His heart grew heavier with each step he took away from her.

At the base of the winding stairs, he beckoned a serving maid forward from where she wove around his men seated at the trestle tables.

She dipped her head as she approached him.

"There is a lady making use of my chamber. Ensure she is given adequate clothing, a meal and a bath."

"Aye, sir." She hurried away.

He stepped across the great hall and entered the chief's solar. His brother stood near the hearth, his hair an unruly mess and his fur vest damp with the morning dew. He clasped Colin's shoulder. "I see you rode hard through the night."

"Aye, I left Neil watching Mingary. What's this I hear about you bringing a lass into the keep?"

"I fished Lila Cunningham from the sea and have offered her my aid in finding her grandmother. Mistress Jean journeyed through here a month past. Do you recall her?"

"I do. She spent a great deal of time with Margaret." His brows drew together. "Lila? That is the name inscribed on your coin."

"The old woman's prophecy has come true. Lila also holds an identical charm to mine, one her grandmother gifted her after receiving it from a fortuneteller." He reached into his pocket and palmed his charm. It hummed with warmth, alleviating a touch of the dark mood that had invaded him since leaving Lila upstairs. "Some form of magic has brought her to me from the future, the year twenty-fourteen, and since her arrival, the two of us have had visions."

"Twenty-fourteen? That's over four-hundred years from now. How is that possible?"

"I cannae say. I only know there is magic at work. Our bond is strong."

"You must take care. The clan wouldnae understand." With

a concerned look, Colin scraped out a chair from under the table littered with the seneschal's accounts and sat.

"Aye, neither of us can speak of what I've learnt." He took the seat opposite. "What news do you bring from Tobermory?"

"MacIan continues to build his ranks. A birlinn bearing Angus MacDonald's flag arrived at Mingary the first night I arrived. It remains berthed at their sea-gate."

"Then it appears MacIan intends to have his MacDonald kin aid him." No surprise, yet not news he wished to hear with their ranks so severely depleted from their battle on Islay. "Readying our men has become imperative."

"Which means you'll no' have time to find your lady's grandmother with what's about to come."

"Aye, she can wait." He'd certainly never allow her to travel with the danger of war in the air, not when she was his to care for.

His clan and Duart must come first.

* * * *

"Hector, show yourself now." An anxious female voice filtered through the window.

Lila flung the wooden shutters open.

Below, a woman with long locks of red-gold raced through the inner courtyard, her red velvet skirts flapping behind her. She braced her hands against the trunk of the towering tree right under her window. Peering upward, she searched through the thick branches sweeping the side of the castle. "I know you're up there, Hector. Please, this isnae the time for play."

"I'm keeping an eye out for Father." A muffled voice called back from somewhere within the dense golden foliage. "He promised he'd come home. I'll see him better from here, Mother."

"I've explained he's in Edinburgh. 'Tis too far away to see."

"Why did the king have to steal him?" The leaves rustled

and a lad with a mop of red curls and big blue eyes crawled out along the branch leading toward her. He glanced at her then wobbled. "Who are you?"

"I'm Lila, and be careful." She wedged sideways out the window and offered him a hand. "Let me help you."

"I need Calum." He clawed the branch. "He'll fetch Father home. He's no' afraid of the king."

"Hector!" The woman clutched her chest. "Down now. This second."

"I—I—" He tried to back up but his arms shook.

"Wait. I'll be right there." Lila swung her legs over the stone windowsill then shimmied onto the branch. The child must be no more than seven, and far too young to be climbing trees of this height. She crawled toward him. "I'll help you find Calum."

"I miss Father." Tears swam in his eyes.

"I'm sorry your father's not here." She grasped him around the waist.

"Hector, I'll be right back with Calum." The woman dashed into the keep.

"How do you know Calum?" A spark of curiosity crossed his face.

"Last night, he rescued me." She held the boy close.

"From this tree?"

"No." She smiled. "The loch. I was out swimming, and got into some trouble."

"Calum's teaching me to swim. He's strong."

"Hector. Lila. Neither of you move." Calum jogged across the courtyard and swung up onto the lowest branch. He scaled the tree, and on the bough next to theirs, eased across then lowered to his haunches. "As nice a day as it is for tree climbing, you two shouldnae be out here."

"S-sorry." Hector launched himself at Calum and he caught the boy and sat him beside him. "Lila said you rescued her too."

"Aye, it appears 'tis what I do best. Now, no more tree

climbing for you."

"I miss Father. Mother does too."

"We all do." He ruffled the boy's red hair. "He'll return soon. The king cannae keep him forever."

"Calum, please send him down." Hector's mother twisted her hands in her skirts.

"He's coming, Margaret." He tucked a loose shirttail into the boy's breeches then turned him around. "Crawl, but take care. We'll speak more about your father once you're down."

"I'll be careful." He snuck back along the branch, climbed down then dropped into Margaret's waiting arms.

Margaret smiled at her. "Thank you. Lila is it?"

"Yes."

"Jean Cunningham spoke of you."

"She did? I'm coming down too."

Calum grasped her from behind before she could move. "Nay, you're no' dressed."

"Calum's right," Margaret called. "I'll be up shortly, right after I've taken care of Hector." She turned to her son, hooked an arm around his shoulders then led him back into the keep.

"Inside with you now." Calum spread his hands around her waist and angled her toward the window.

Together they crawled inside to a buzz of activity. During her tree climbing, her bath and meal had arrived. Two lads in loose brown tunics poured steaming pails of water into a tub set before the hearth, and a maid with a gown in hand, draped it over the end of the bed. They bustled out and shut the door behind them.

"I ordered this for you." Calum pulled out a chair before his desk where a tray had been laid.

"Thank you. Tree climbing certainly fires the appetite." She sat, lifted the small bowl of honey and swirled it over top of the hot oats. "It's been ages since I've had porridge. I have a terrible habit of sleeping in, so I usually grab a snack bar and eat on the run." She slid a spoonful into her mouth. Delicious, and it tasted exactly like Nanna used to make on those cold winter mornings. She held out a second spoonful for him. "Would you like some?"

He caught her hand, brought her spoon to his mouth then slid it sensuously between his lips. "Where do you run to?"

"The train station. In the future we have these big steel contraptions that run on long metal tracks and carry passengers. People all over the city ride the trains to work."

"You dinnae ride a horse?"

"Sadly, I've never even touched one. There are far faster means of getting about than on a horse." She took another spoonful. "What news did your brother bring?"

"MacIan's ranks have grown with the aid of his MacDonald kin. With an attack so close at hand, I must prepare my men." He brushed his thumb along her cheek. "Which means my plans have changed. You must remain here until 'tis safe to search for your grandmother."

"I can't. I don't know how long I have in this time. Every minute counts."

"Aye, though remain you will." He stood and dropped a kiss on the top of her head. "I'll leave you to your bath afore the water cools and return at midday after training. You'll stay here, within Duart's walls." He strode out the door and shut it quietly behind him.

She'd enjoy her bath then speak with Margaret. She'd remain only until she knew where to go.

She peeled off his borrowed shirt, stepped into the tub and eased her head back against the rim. The water sloshed to her chin, and the alluring fragrance of roses wafted in the steam. Heavenly. She scooped the soap and washed away the salt still clinging to her skin from the night before.

A knock sounded on the door. "Lila, 'tis Margaret."

"Come in." Not wanting to miss this conversation, she slid under the bubbles, covering herself adequately.

Margaret walked in with a posy of lavender in her hand. "I apologize for disturbing your bath."

"No, we need to speak. I'm eager to hear about my grandmother."

"Aye, she said you would come." She set the flowers on the side table then perched on the chair before the fire. "She confided in me."

"How did she know I'd come?" She sloshed water over the rim as she sat up. "Tell me everything."

"Jean spoke of the faraway place you both came from." She clasped her hands in her lap. "And I mean the future, a realm beyond my imagination."

Gosh, Nanna must have trusted Margaret, even though she was married to the MacLean chief. "Keep going."

"Afore I wed Lachlan, I too was a Cunningham as your grandmother was. We're kin." She dipped a finger under the red lace edging of her bodice and freed a gold necklace. The disk dangling from it was engraved with the image of a unicorn, the same mythical creature that graced Nanna's necklace and the Cunningham clan crest. The pendants appeared so similar. "Because of our close ties, we formed a bond of trust, one I would never break."

She rose, and lifting her skirts, knelt at the edge of the tub. "There is folklore surrounding those born under a falling star, that they have stunning silver eyes and magic flowing in their blood. When they make a wish, with all their heart and soul, that wish may be granted."

Nanna had often spun that childhood tale, but she'd never imagined any truth in it. Yet if she and Nanna had been born with magic in their blood, it might explain how they'd both ended up in the past. Her wish had certainly been made with all her heart and soul, and she had silver eyes.

"You're here, and magic brought you did it no'?"

"Yes, I think you're right." She touched Margaret's

keepsake. "How come your pendant looks so much like Nanna's?"

"This necklace was gifted to me by my father, William Cunningham, the sixth Earl of Glencairn. He commissioned one of these keepsakes for each of his five daughters and we received them respectively on our wedding day. 'Tis been a tradition carried down through the generations. Jean acquired hers as an heirloom from her Cunningham father on the day she wed. Look." She turned the trinket over. "Margaret is inscribed on the back of mine."

Yes, and Nanna's was etched with her name. "I miss her."

"She too spoke of missing you." Margaret rubbed her arm. "She left you a message, one I couldnae speak of to another. She said you must no' tell Calum that you're from the MacIan clan. Jean used the name Cunningham, and you must use it too. She also spoke of the fortuneteller who gave her your charm. The old woman told her that the past must be set to rights. That's why you're both here."

"Calum was told the same thing." Goodness, she needed to find that fortuneteller.

"Come, the water cools and you're shivering." Margaret passed her a drying cloth.

"Why didn't Nanna wait here for me if she knew I would come?" She dried herself then picked up the sapphire gown the maid had left and eased it over her head. The soft folds shimmered down her hips and swished to her ankles.

"Duart was no' her home."

"Yes, but we don't have any home in this time period. Waiting here would've been best." She laced the front stays to the top of the square-cut neckline trimmed with a lacy ribbon, then donned the matching slippers.

"Come. Your hair will dry quicker afore the fire, and I'll explain further." Margaret patted the wooden chair and Lila sat. "Jean was told by the fortuneteller there were two charms linked through time, as was their true holders' souls. That's why you and Jean both arrived here first, where Calum holds the other charm."

So Calum was like the magnet that had drawn Nanna and her to the same place and point in time. Calum too had said they were bound, and after only a short time in his company, she believed.

"You need to know your grandmother awaits you." Margaret picked up a brush from the side table, separated her hair into sections and combed. "You must follow in Jean's path."

"To where?" The moment she knew, she'd go.

"Look into your heart for the answer." Margaret smiled. "Deep inside, you know exactly where she's gone. Where do the MacIans reside?"

"Mingary," she whispered.

"Aye, you will find your grandmother in the home of your ancestors. That too is where you need to be in order to set your past to rights."

"Then I have to leave, immediately." Except Calum had already said she must remain here. "But it'll have to be in secret."

"Aye, if you're bound to Calum as strongly as Jean has said, then you must leave without his knowledge." She set the brush down. "I will aid you as I did Jean."

"Thank you. That means the world to me. What's the easiest route to take from here to Mingary?"

"By way of the forest path. It meanders alongside the coastline toward the tip of Mull. Once you reach Tobermory, you can hire one of the fishermen to sail you across the sound. They willnae wish to make landfall for long, but 'tis a short mile across the sea, no more. I have my own coin. I'll give you what you need."

"I'll find a way to repay you." Her heart heaved at the thought of leaving Calum. They'd had so little time together. Oh, but Nanna was close. All she'd ever learnt was at her knee, and now it would only be a matter of days before she saw her again.

Not a soul could keep her from this journey, not even Calum.

"I have to see him before I go." She owed him her life.

"I'll take you. The men will have left for the training yard."

Lila retrieved her charm from the bedside nightstand and gripped it tight.

A journey into MacIan land would be treacherous for Calum. Going alone was her only option. This was her mission, not his, whether their charms and souls were bound or not.

Chapter 4

Margaret guided Lila down the winding stairs and into the great hall.

Within a wide arched stone fireplace, sparks flared, and firelight shimmered across the hefty clan shield hanging over it. So beautiful. The silver edge, embedded with diamonds, rubies and yellow sapphires, gave proof of just how much wealth this clan held. The MacLeans had certainly survived and thrived as her clan had not.

They passed two maids clearing the trenchers away, and a large brown-haired dog guzzling scraps from under the trestle tables.

Outside in the bailey, the sun shone and she breathed the fresh sea air in.

"'Tis a short walk to the training yard at the tip of the loch. 'Twill no' take long." Margaret snuck her through the arched gates and into the outer courtyard. The glittering waters of the sound beckoned, and so close lay Ardnamurchan.

They followed the stony path.

Near the stables, a gangly-legged lad in loosely belted pants brushed a sleek black warhorse. Beyond him, two armed warriors mounted their steeds then galloped across the moors toward the forest. "It's awful you must live like this, so on guard all the time."

"There is naught we can do to halt this feud, no' when Lachlan fights to right the past wrongs done to him."

"What wrongs are those?" The path weaved uphill, and she lifted her skirts out of the dust.

"Lachlan's father, in the short five years he was chief, gambled away his lands on Islay, but they were unfairly lost to him. 'Tis why he's so determined to get the Rhinns back."

"If that's so, then why doesn't he simply take his case to the king? It would have saved on the whole being captured thing."

"He'll never accede to the king, no' in anyway. To do so, would be accepting the king's rule over our isle."

Since it was the late 1500s, the king had to be James VI, one of the greatest kings of all times. What she'd read about him at the museum had intrigued her. Because of his birth, he'd successfully united the kingdoms of England and Scotland at the turn of the coming century. He'd led with determination during his long reign. A shame she hadn't read more about this particular feud. That would've been helpful.

They made the top rise and she raised a hand to her brow. Duart sat prominently at the point where the Sound of Mull intersected with Loch Linne and the Firth of Lorne. Land rose from the water in every direction. A very favorable position for a stronghold with its unhindered views.

"If you look to the south you can see the isles of Jura and Islay." Margaret plucked a yellow flower from the lush grass and tucked it behind her ear. "Lachlan holds the northern half of Jura. That he has never lost."

"Where are the Rhinns located?"

"There on Islay's west."

"It's close."

"Aye, we usually receive fair warning when our enemy sails these waterways." She pointed toward a cluster of trees where beyond the clashing of steel against steel rung through the air. "The men are down there, where they can also keep watch over it all."

"Then it's time for me to see Calum." She strode along the thinning, scrub-lined path. At the edge of the loch, a hundred shirtless warriors wielded swords in a battle of strength against one another. Another hundred swam toward a small island in the middle of the waterway. "That's some training."

"Our enemies dinnae lie idle, and neither may we."

Among the half-naked men, Calum swung his two-handed claymore down on his opponent's. His shoulders and arms were thick, strong, and packed with muscle. A healthy sheen of sweat glistened across his glorious abs. He shoved forward and the force of his move sent the warrior he fought against stumbling backward. So impressive.

"Mother!" Hector raced down the trail toward them, his red hair a bright beacon of color amongst the green of the moors.

"Slow down or you'll trip and fall." Margaret caught him as he plowed into her. "Oomph."

"I have a message for you from Betsie." His breath came hard and fast. "She said Bethag fell and cries for you."

"Oh dear." She spun and faced Lila. "My daughter. She's learning to walk. I must go and see she's well. I'll return soon and"—she leaned in and squeezed her hands—"sneak your bag out as I do."

"Thank you. I must leave without anyone seeing."

"'Twill be done." Margaret hurried after Hector.

One quick goodbye with Calum, and then she'd be away.

She threaded through the battling men, all far too intent on killing each other, as if they were each other's mortal enemy. If this was training, she shuddered to think what an actual battle would look like. She darted through then fell in behind the one she was after. "Calum, I—"

He jerked around. "Lila? What are you—"

"Behind you, Calum."

The warrior he battled swung his sword.

Calum whirled, barely catching his opponent's blow. "Get back, Lila."

A blade whistled past her ear, and hot air pulsed all around. She was blocked on every side. "Get back to where?"

"Hold onto me." Calum scooped her against him then dodged through his warring men until they reached the edge of the flat.

"I'm so sorry." She plastered her face against his chest, her heart beating so loud it pounded in her ears. "I didn't know that would happen."

"They cannae see any but their opponent when their blood roars for the fight." He gripped her hand and tugged her into the thick copse of surrounding pine trees. Nesting birds twittered within the highest branches. "How did you manage to slip past the tower guardsman?"

"I was with Margaret and we didn't have an issue. I needed to come. I had to see you."

"Then speak." He slid his claymore into the sheath strapped to his bare back.

Oh, now she had to find a way to say goodbye without actually coming out and saying it. "You left so quickly this morning." Okay, that was a good start.

"That is hardly an adequate reason for the risk you just took with your life." He backed her against a wide trunk, his gaze dropping to her lips.

"I wanted to thank you for saving my life and pulling me from the loch."

"You did that last eve." He dipped his head, urged her lips apart and from one heart-stopping breath to the next, swarmed her senses with a ferocious kiss. Every inch of her sizzled, burned and throbbed.

"Once didn't seem enough," she said when he finally eased

back.

"My apologies. I had to kiss you." He caressed her sides, roamed down and scooped her bottom. He lifted her higher and pressed his hard length against her belly. "Do you feel our connection?"

"Yes." She seized his powerful biceps and held on. "I'm not sure what we're going to do about it though."

"I do." He kissed her again, so deeply their breath mingled as one, his hardness a hot brand that made her tingle all over. Then he cupped her breast and thumbed the peak through her gown. "In the cave, I saw your beautiful hair spread like black silk over my tartan. I've wished since for that vision to come true."

"You have a wicked way with words." She tangled her fingers in his hair and reclaimed his mouth.

* * * *

Calum groaned as Lila pressed her breast more fully into his palm. He stroked the pebbled peak of her nipple. Her breast was lush, and he ached for more. Carefully, he swept her bodice to the side then eased his hand in. The lace edging slid sensuously over the back of his hand as he filled his palm with her warm flesh. "Aye we will be one as I've seen. 'Tis only a matter of time."

Heat surged through his blood and dove straight to his cock. He immersed himself in the heat of her, drinking in her sweet taste.

He wanted more, and not just to have his hand against her. He loosened the ribbon and eased her gown over her shoulder. One pink and luscious nipple beckoned. He rolled his tongue around the tip and sucked.

"Calum." She moaned and arched into him. "That feels so good."

His vision resurged, of his plaid pooled around her hips. He wished to slide that last obstacle away and love her fully as he should. They were bound, and in the deepest sense. 'Twas as if she were a part of him, and now she'd returned to claim her rightful place in his life. He moved to her other breast and tasted the tight bud. Perfect.

She broke their kiss and looked into his eyes. "Where's that cave? Is it close?"

"There are caves all over Mull, and I've no' seen which one might be ours." The clamoring of weapons rang in his ears. Damn. How had he forgotten his men trained just beyond the trees? When he made love to his woman, he'd give her a night of pure pleasure, not a fast coupling in the woods. "We need to wait."

"We do?" She shook her head as if trying to clear it. "Oh, of course we do. You're in the middle of training, and I was in the middle of, well, never mind. You're right. We should wait."

"Is there more you need? Have you spoken to Margaret?"

"Yes, I did." She adjusted her gown, covering the luscious golden skin he'd exposed. "She knows about my grandmother, and that we're both from the future. Nanna told her, being that they were Cunningham kin."

"Margaret never spoke a word." Mayhap she feared for Jean if she had. Other than Colin, he too would never tell another of Lila's time travel. "Is she aware of where your grandmother journeyed to?" A question he would have asked Margaret himself at midday once he returned.

"Calum!" The shout came from one of his men.

"How about we talk about this later. I should have waited at the castle as you said." She rubbed his chest.

"Aye, I'll escort you back to the keep."

"No, I've kept you from your training long enough." She ducked under his arm and around the brush. "The castle is close. I can manage the short walk alone."

"I'll accompany you all the same." His wee charm certainly liked to have her way, though so did he.

"Seriously, you go swing that sword of yours about and ensure no one tries to take your head off again." She strode out of the forest and into the meadow, her long black hair swaying from hip to hip.

He wanted to pull her back into his arms, the urge the strongest he'd had. 'Twas too dangerous to let her out of his sight. "Lila, wait."

"Margaret's expecting me." She blew him a kiss then picked up her pace. "Be careful when you return to the fight."

Something was afoot. Lila had come to him and now she couldn't leave quick enough. He yanked the horn from his side, blew long and loud then called for the change. The warriors on land would switch with those in the loch. Icy water would clear their battle lust.

Bent, catching his breath, Colin waved him over. "There you are. 'Twas I who called out. Was that Lila?"

"Aye." He passed him the horn. "I'll see her safely back to the keep. Oversee the men until I return."

"Is all well?"

"She thinks to dismiss her need for protection."

"Go. I'll remain here."

"My thanks." He clapped Colin on the shoulder then followed after Lila. His protection of her would be absolute, a fact she would soon learn.

* * * *

Lila lifted her cumbersome sapphire skirts and ran. How could she have let Calum's kisses sidetrack her like that? Nanna came first. Goodness, she had no idea how this time travel worked or how long she might be stuck in the past. Every minute counted. So the tower guard wouldn't see her, she veered off the trail then snuck down to the loch and hid behind the sand dunes.

"Lila." Margaret raced alongside a thick clump of bushes, keeping herself hidden too. "I packed a bag for you. It includes your strange suit of black from Calum's chamber." She skidded over the dunes. "Why are we hiding? Did your farewell no' go well?"

"Calum insisted he escort me back, and he may follow. Thank you for these things, but I'll only need what I came with. There's no time to delay." She hauled off her gown and tugged the wetsuit on.

"You're going to swim across the sound?" Margaret grasped her shoulders. "Nay, allow me to organize a horse."

"No, Calum will find out. I'll be fine in the water. I swim all the time and I'll rest as needed." She swiped her charm from her gown's pocket and shoved it into her zippered pouch.

"I cannae believe you must swim." Margaret glanced toward the rise. "If there's no other choice, then swim alongside Mull's coastline. Only cross the waters once you reach Tobermory. 'Tis the safest course."

"I'll do that, and don't worry about me." She shoved her flippers on and jammed her mask into place. "I told Calum we spoke, and that you knew I was from the future."

"He'll question me." She fluttered a hand over her mouth. "What shall I say?"

"Tell him this was my choice. I don't want him to worry, or for you to get into any trouble. But he can't stop me once I'm gone, so speak as you will. It won't matter." She hugged Margaret. "Thank you again for your help. I wouldn't have been able to get away like this without you."

"I will always be here to aid you should you need it."

"No wonder Nanna trusted you." She released her then shuffled backward into the surf. Along the hilly rise, Calum ran, his dark hair whipping in the breeze as he tore along the trail toward the castle.

"Go quickly," Margaret called then ducked, remaining hidden.

She dove into the cold waters of the loch. Her heart ached for the time she and Calum would never have together, but

Nanna needed her. She wouldn't fail in her mission to reach Mingary.

* * * *

Pain slammed through Calum's chest and he stumbled to his knees in the thick grass. 'Twas as if someone had taken a spear and thrust it right through his heart.

Toward the sound, something sleek and black disappeared within the tumbling waves.

With one hand on the ground, he shoved to his feet then raced toward the loch. He skidded over the sand dunes and tumbled into Margaret. "What are you doing here?"

Tears misted her eyes. "I'm sorry. Lila had to go."

"Where?"

"I—I—"

"Tell me, Margaret. We're bound in a way I cannae explain. I need her. Which way?"

"T-Tobermory, then she intended to swim across the sound to Ardnamurchan. 'Tis where Jean Cunningham traveled to." Tears trickled freely down her cheeks. "She didnae wish for you to worry, but you must let her go. Her journey cannae wait."

"She's mine to protect." From the damned sea no less. On his life, he'd find her, no matter her wish to leave him. Hell, Ardnamurchan. He'd never allow her to travel to the enemy's land.

* * * *

Lila pushed on, swimming at a good pace as the hours trickled by. Seagulls circling overhead squawked, and a playful seal pup darted around. The waters teemed with life, but with each stroke she took, her heart sank deeper. Leaving Calum shouldn't be this hard, and this bond they had shouldn't hold this much power over her.

She swam past the odd village nestled close to the water's edge, but took extra care and kept her distance as fishermen cast their nets from their skiffs.

63

Soon the high tide moved with the setting of the sun, the current flowing swifter into shore. Her chilled muscles ached, and wearily, she rode a cresting wave into a darkened, secluded cove. The perfect spot to rest for the night.

She trudged out then hands on her knees, dragged in a deep breath. Moonlight flickered over the rocky beach and shimmered across the treetops. The wind blasted through and she rubbed her arms with numb fingers.

At the edge of the beach where it met the forest, a stream gurgled into the sea. She lumbered toward it, lowered herself to her knees and shakily scooped water. She drank and the cold rush of liquid hit her empty belly and sent shudders raking through her. She swayed and grappled for the stream's edge.

Too late. A rock loomed and she hit it hard.

She clutched her head as black spots danced before her eyes.

* * * *

Calum urged his black destrier faster along the narrow forest path edging the cliffs. Below, the sea roared and crashed against the jagged rock wall. Lila was out there in that dark squall when she should be tucked safely in his bed. How had he allowed her to escape? And how had not one of the fishermen he'd stopped to speak to thus far, not seen any sign of her?

White-hot terror suddenly cut through him, their connection gaining in strength. Something had happened to her, and he'd felt the razor sharp blow to the depths of his soul.

Fisting his horse's reins, he burst out of the forest and plunged down the hillside toward an isolated bay. At the mouth of a stream, the incoming tide washed over something.

Hell. 'Twas Lila.

Face down, her unmistakable silky black hair floated around her.

He slammed his knees into his steed, jumped a fallen tree across his path and raced.

No one would take Lila from him.

Never again.

* * * *

Lila's head shattered with pain, and her back throbbed as if someone beat on it.

Thunder pounded in her ears, and her name echoed all around.

Why was Nanna yelling at her? And why was her voice so deep?

She tried to call back, managed a croaky, "Stop."

"Breathe, damn it." Muscled arms wrapped around her and flattened her against a hot, hard chest. Definitely not Nanna.

She forced her eyes open and the haze cleared. A golden gaze, filled with fear and relief drilled into hers. "Calum?"

"I have to keep you safe from the sea." He smothered her in his warmth.

"You do?" That sounded right, only where was Nanna? "I'm so c-cold."

"I'll start a fire and have you warm afore too long."

"Nanna's l-left the windows open." She nuzzled his neck and the heat of his skin scorched her frozen nose. Oh, he smelled delicious, that fresh scent of his one she wanted to roll around in. "What am I doing here?"

"You escaped me, and it'll no' happen again." He cradled her in his arms as he carried her and whistled. A horse whinnied and he grabbed the animal's reins as it appeared out of the gloomy dark.

"You're going to be in so much trouble." She jabbed his chest. "Nanna doesn't allow horses in the house."

"Your grandmother isnae here." He mumbled something she missed then said more clearly, "There's a cave right alongside this cliff."

"You mean our cave?" Her muddled thoughts were slowly clearing. "The one you saw in your vision?"

"Aye, it must be. Our future has been foretold." He pressed his lips to hers, sending another blast of heat through her. She itched to get closer, to seek the ultimate contact. He was so hot, only he broke the kiss as he walked with her into the trees.

Brush scraped against her shoulders as he looped his horse's reins to a low branch. He strode along a narrow ledge of rock, and the sea's cold spray pelted into her. She burrowed, her cheek mashed against his damp shirt. "H-hurry."

"Almost there." He strode into the cave. "We'll remain close to the entrance so the smoke from the fire can escape."

"A fire sounds good." The gritty walls held a slight odor, but the wind was gone. She longed for more warmth.

"I need to collect some wood." Carefully, he set her down beside the wall, unraveled his plaid and wrapped her in it. Hunkered down, he tipped her chin toward him and looked into her eyes. "You appear more lucid. Dinnae move. I'll be as quick as I can."

"You said fire, so I'm staying." She curled onto her side, his tartan wrapped tight. "Could you grab me some hot chocolate too, please. That'd really help warm me up."

"Mayhap I spoke too soon. Rest." He kissed her, his lips so gentle on hers. Then he disappeared into the dark.

She yawned. Rest sounded wonderful.

* * * *

Hoping to catch a small creature, Calum set a snare then collected twigs and a couple of logs. He snatched his bag, spare plaid, and the sack of clothes Margaret had packed for Lila from his horse. Margaret's words returned to him. Lila was headed to Ardnamurchan. His woman had spoken of his enemy's land when he'd first rescued her from Duart Bay, though why her grandmother had intended to travel there, he couldn't fathom.

At the cave, he knelt and rested his cheek near Lila's lips. Her breath fluttered across his skin and relief poured through him. If he'd been any later in finding her, he'd have lost her.

Quickly, he dug a small pit in the sandy dirt. He pulled the stringy bark off a log, struck flint with his dirk, and coaxed the sparks to life. He built the fire into a crackling blaze with the twigs and wood.

"Mmm, Calum." She wriggled and stretched.

"Aye, I'm here." He spread his spare plaid closer to the heat of the flames, scooped her up and laid her in front of him. With his body curved around hers, he tried to share as much of his own heat as he could.

"That's good. Sooo good."

"You should have remained at Duart." He tucked a lock of her black hair behind her ear then wiped grit from her cheeks and chin.

"Sorry, what? Did you get the hot chocolate?"

"You're teasing me?" Aye, she was, going by the mischievous tilt to her lips. "What is this hot chocolate you speak of?"

"You have to try it. You take chocolate powder and stir it into frothy milk then toss a big gooey marshmallow on top. Delicious. The waitress at my local coffee shop makes the best ones." She pushed her hands from the confines of his tartan and wiggled her fingers before the flames. "After I fell into the stream I thought Nanna was here, or I was back home, or something. Remind me to never drink icy water on an empty stomach again."

"What I'll do is never allow you to swim in the loch again."

She squirmed around. "I couldn't stay at Duart, not when I have to get to Ardnamurchan."

"Margaret told me where you'd gone. Why do you believe your grandmother left for MacIan's territory?"

"If I told you, you'd get angry, and right when I want to show you some appreciation for saving my life." Her silver eyes lit. "Want to know how?"

"By showing me your heart shaped mole?" Nay, he

shouldn't encourage her. She needed to rest.

"I missed you, Calum." She leaned in and kissed him. "After I swam away, I felt as if I'd left part of me behind. Each mile dragged."

"You willnae leave me again." He brushed his lips across hers, wanting desperately to imbibe further and drink in her sweet taste. An urge to show her exactly how much he'd missed her burned through him. Aye, this was their cave, the one where he would—damn it, she was still weak and needed to conserve her strength.

"That mole on my belly"—she melted against him—"I want you to see it. Can you help me take this wetsuit off? I want to feel more of the fire's heat on my skin."

"I—I set the snare."

"Then I'd say it caught me." Her sweet mouth lifted and he traced her plump lower lip.

No more. He had to get out of here. He shot to his feet and dived out of the cave.

"Hey, where are you going? That's not the kind of snare I meant, mister."

"I'll return with food," he called back. "If you wish to change, there's clothing in the sack Margaret packed for you."

Her sigh followed him into the dark as he marched on. From his pocket, he seized his charm and smoothed over the inscription.

Perhaps he should wish for more visions, so he'd be forewarned if Lila ever attempted to leave him again.

A soft snap dinged from the direction of his snare. He tramped across to it, removed the rabbit, took it down to the water's edge and skinned and cleaned it. Determined to have his questions answered, he returned to the cave.

Lila sat cross-legged before the fire, her wetsuit discarded near their bags. His plaid was still wrapped around her but her golden shoulders and bare back were exposed where it looped down. She wore naught underneath as his vision had shown. Then she glanced at him and smiled. "Nice catch."

"You didnae change." He chose some sturdy sticks and fashioned a spit for the rabbit.

"Would you hold me?"

"Nay." The longing in her voice almost turned him from his task. He had cold oatcakes in his bag, but she needed warm food in her belly. He jammed the rabbit into place and set it to cook over the fire.

"Please, Calum. I don't care for this distance you're now putting between us."

"You began with the distance when you left me." He removed his sword-belt, propped it within arm's reach against the damp wall then dropped down beside her. "Tell me about Ardnamurchan."

"That would be the piece of land across the sound, and holding me requires the involvement of your arms."

"Answer my question." Giving in, he lifted her up, set her in front and nestled her back against his chest, ensuring the tartan was wrapped tight around her. Gently, he smoothed out her drying hair. The strands shimmered midnight-blue in the firelight and slid like silk through his fingers.

"It feels so right being here with you, like this moment was meant to be." She twisted around and faced him, her gaze hot on his. "Except it causes a complication."

"There is no complication. We belong together." He nuzzled her neck, blowing warm air across her flesh. Hell, what was he doing?

"This thing between us is moving too fast, only I can't deny it exists. Life is too short, and I don't want another day to go by without experiencing what you've seen."

"I saw only your upper body. 'Twas likely naught."

"Or it was something." She kissed him, long and slowly. "I've never shown anyone my upper body before. I want you to be my first." She rubbed against him, her beaded nipples poking his chest through the tartan. He itched for the ultimate contact with her, and his cock strained to get closer. It would stab through his leather trews if he didn't do something about it.

Chapter 5

Heat and energy pulsed through Lila when not long ago she'd been exhausted and chilled to the bone. She'd waited a lifetime for this moment. Calum had saved her twice from the sea, and though he was from the enemy clan, his heart was pure. She desperately wanted to join with him.

"Calum, show me everything you saw in your vision."

"Aye, everything." He released the plaid still covering her. The soft wool slid over her bare skin and pooled at her hips. With painstaking slowness, he grazed a finger from between her breasts to her belly, his sensual touch starting a pulse point fluttering in her below.

"I really like how you touch me."

"I like it more." He skimmed his hands over her waist and pressed his lips to her belly. He kissed her, right over her heart shaped mole. "Beautiful, and just as I saw it."

"How about you show me your star shaped birthmark?" She tickled down his side and around to his right cheek. "It was about here, wasn't it?"

"Aye, though I intend a long loving of your body first." He laid her back on his plaid, eased her breasts together and licked one nipple. The lazy stroke of his tongue sent a bolt of pleasure to her core.

"I never want to forget this night."

"I'll ensure it." He swirled around the tip then sucked her nipple deep into his mouth. She couldn't halt her hips from pushing against his. He'd awakened her body, and she wanted more. His shirt. It had to go. She gripped the hem and hauled it over his head. His glorious abs and pecs gleamed under the firelight.

She clutched his broad shoulders then caressed his biceps as he devoured her breasts.

"I need more, Lila." He cupped her bottom and brought her tight against him.

"Then a good start would be to get you completely naked." She loosened the ties of his pants, shoved the dark leather down his thighs and off. Oh yes. His cock sprang free and brushed his belly. Her stomach tightened in expectation.

"I want to feel your heart beating against mine."

"My heart's racing a little out of time." She craved his touch. Her warrior was beyond beautiful, and this bond, which tied them together, was one she hadn't a hope of dismissing. His body too, every hard and defined inch of him. She wanted, desperately. "Let me touch you."

"Later. I've waited too long." He dipped his fingers between them and glided along the inside of her thigh. "Spread your legs, my wee charm."

She eased them apart, eager and needy for his touch. "Whatever you do, don't stop."

"Naught will halt me now." He swept his hand over her entrance, his intimate touch a sweet caress. Then he plunged one finger inside and stroked deep, curling into a spot that had her straining for more. Hands on her hips, he slowly, carefully, moved between her legs and nudged his cock along her slick folds. "Do you trust me?"

"Yes, hurry. I'm burning up for your touch."

He returned to her mouth and kissed her, diverting her thoughts with each delicious kiss. Then he pushed against the barrier, tore through and plunged inside.

She held on piercingly tight as he stretched her to exquisite fullness. She wanted to speak, but the way they were joined touched her so deeply, as if their very souls had merged.

"We're one, and none shall ever tear us apart." He stared into her eyes, his gaze restless.

"This is like nothing I could've imagined." She grasped his butt and wrapped her quivering legs around him. "Show me a night of pleasure."

"Aye." With one hand on her hip, he eased up then slid with tortuous slowness back in.

"Faster, Calum." He increased his pace and she couldn't hold back her moan. Her thoughts were consumed by him as he pounded, hard and deep. Her body rose to meet his, and he took her frantically, as if struggling to contain his own desire. Moving with him, she only wanted this magical moment to never end.

"Let go, Lila. I'm right here with you."

"Only with you." Every one of his kisses and caresses had her poised on the edge, flooding her with more sensation than she could stand. She let go and soared, her inner muscles tightening as she bucked against him. Pleasure overflowed her body and swept her into a sea of shimmering stars, the most exhilarating experience.

Filled completely, he spilled his seed deep, his release as violent as hers. Body and soul, her connection to him transcended time. And she came, meeting each of his strokes until she could take no more, until his very scent became embedded into her skin.

"You're my charm," he whispered, his heart drumming against hers as he slumped on top, completely spent. "There is no escaping me now."

* * * *

The meaty aroma of cooked rabbit wafted through the air and stirred Calum from his slumber. He rolled toward the fire, removed the meat from the spit then nudged Lila awake. "Our food is ready. Are you hungry?"

"Very." She stretched and eased up, her beautiful breasts on full display and tempting him almost beyond his endurance.

Nay, he couldn't allow her to distract him when they needed to speak. She'd waylaid this conversation already. He tore the meat into small slivers then slipped a morsel between her lips. "In the morn, we return to Duart, and you're no' to flee from me again."

"You're responsible for an entire clan, and that's where you need to be. Nanna needs me. I have to continue on."

"Your grandmother left of her own accord and is likely well. MacIan could attack at any moment, and I cannae have you wandering right into the heart of the battle." He stroked the back of her head. "You must remain safe, until the threat has passed."

"There's no threat to me, not since I'm a Cunningham." She pressed her hand against his chest, right over his heart. "I've crossed centuries to find her. She's all I have, and she expects me to follow her."

"You're all I have, and she wouldnae wish you to risk your life. When you left, it near wrenched my soul in two."

"I can't wait for this feud to end."

"All I ask is that you give me some time." He tipped her onto her back, prepared to do all he must to ensure she understood. "Ardnamurchan is the enemy's territory. I'll never allow you to pass into their land alone. The danger is too great."

She shoved against his shoulders, rolled him onto his back and straddled his legs. "For starters, I can see I'll need to be more forceful with you."

His cock throbbed at her words. Aye, though he would be forceful first. From his tartan, he tore a strip off, clasped his right hand with her right, and wrapped his plaid around their hands.

Bound together, he would ensure she was a Cunningham no more. This was right.

"What are you doing?" She wriggled her fingers. "You can't be this worried I'm going to get away?"

"'Tis a handfast. The vows we speak now will bind us together as man and wife for a year and a day, and as soon as Brother John returns from Tobermory, we'll be wed proper. I need to know you're mine, in every single way."

"You want to get hitched? Like right now? While we're in the middle of an argument? Did you see us doing this in your vision?"

"Nay, I never saw this, only your mole. Now, let's begin." He cleared his throat. "I, Calum William MacLean, of Mull, pledge my troth to Lila Cunningham. With this handfast, I take her as my wife for the next year and a day." He tightened his grip on her hand. "Speak your vow, love."

"I can't believe—"

"I'll accept naught less." He spread her folds below then slid his cock deep into the heart of her welcoming channel.

"Oooh, we're going to have to talk about your need to take control." Panting, she moved up and down.

"If you wish, you may take some control now, but when it comes to your safety, my decision stands firm." Grinning, he rocked his hips. "I look forward to the consummation."

"You're already covering that quite nicely, and regardless of your clear attempt at coercion, I can handle you, no matter you're a sixteenth century man." She moved faster. "I, Lila, of Australia, pledge my troth to Calum William MacLean. With this handfast, I take him as my husband for the next year and a day." Her eyes smoldered, making his blood pound all the harder. "What do you wish for next?"

"We seal the vows with a kiss."

"Oh, you are wicked." She leaned over and kissed him, so possessively his cock throbbed on the verge of release.

Wicked? She was the wicked one.

He rolled her onto her back, reclaimed her lips and plundered. Filling her in every way, he made her his wife.

"I love you, Lila, my charm." He moved, thrusting as deep as she could take him. "You've returned to me, and I willnae have you leave again."

"I see images." She gripped his butt and pushed her hips upward. "Oh, you're about to make me fly."

The same vision surged to the forefront of his mind. Lila, her legs wrapped around him, their right hands joined by his MacLean plaid and the two of them lost in their love. Buried deep within her, and his heartbeat thumping against hers, he didn't hold back. With one decisive flick of his finger over her clit, he made her come, so staggeringly fast.

She cried his name. "I love you, Calum. I always will. Time can never keep us apart."

"Aye, we remain together, forever." He looked deep into her eyes then bellowed as he sank balls-deep inside her. He coated her womb with his seed, pulse after pulse until she'd milked him dry.

"Forceful. It seems I really like forceful." Her eyelids fluttered shut and she sighed with a wide smile.

Aye, his charm possessed him, heart, body and soul.

With not an ounce of strength left, he collapsed and allowed sleep to claim him.

Chapter 6

Waking to Calum's warm breath tickling her ear was the sweetest, as was the heavy weight of his arm across her waist. Sunshine streamed through the opening of their cave and heated Lila's skin. She stretched. "Ouch."

"Where do you hurt?" He tipped her toward him.

"I'm all right. I don't usually sleep on the hard ground, nor do I usually work every muscle in my body until I pass out." Oh, but it had all been totally worth it.

"I'll look you over." His golden eyes heated and said far more.

"I know exactly where your kind of looking will likely lead." She cupped his stubbly jaw and kissed him, one very delicious and rewarding morning kiss. "That's all you're getting for now."

"Aye, we must return afore Colin or my men track me down." He lifted her onto his lap then with his arms around her, worked at loosening the strip of plaid still binding them. Once freed, he rose to his feet and set her on hers. "Dress quickly."

From the sack Calum had brought her, she unfolded a sky blue gown and eased it over her head. The velvet skimmed her hips and fell in a swish to her ankles. She laced the stays to the top of the low ruffled neckline then tied a bow and slid on a pair of thick-soled slippers. Next to her, Calum dressed in a clean shirt and leather pants before strapping his sword belt over his hips.

She had to continue on to Ardnamurchan, whether he liked it or not. "Calum, we need to talk."

"Speak as you will." He traced along the top swell of her breasts then leaned in and kissed her, so sweetly.

"We want to head in opposite directions." Oh, she wanted him to trail his finger lower, but instead of allowing it, she stepped away to the cave's opening. Twenty feet below, the waves washed in and pounded the sheer cliff side.

"I know, love, but for now you must remain with me." He draped his spare plaid over her shoulders then pinned it in place. From his supplies, he passed her a skin of water and an oatcake. "This will have to suffice until we make the village."

Across the choppy waters of the sound, Ardnamurchan's green hills rose into the distance. She nibbled on her oatcake. Nanna was so close, and she couldn't turn back now.

"What are you thinking?" He scraped dirt across the charred remains of their fire.

"I'm considering how I'm going to make you hear me out." She removed her charm from her wetsuit and gripped it. Honesty was all she had left, and they'd spoken their vows. He was her husband.

"If you wish to talk, then do so." He swung their bags over his shoulder. "Though while we ride."

"I'm not returning to Duart, not when I have to find Nanna first."

"She can wait, as this war will no'." He strode to opening. "We ride. Now."

"Calum, I'm not who you think I am. I mean, I am, but I'm not a Cunningham."

"Nay, you're a MacLean now. I ensured it last eve."

"Yes, and I would claim your name with pride, but my grandmother's name is actually Jean MacIan, as was my father's." She'd done it now. Put it all out there. No more secrets.

"You're a—nay." He fisted his hands and shook his head. "Dinnae speak a mistruth to me. You're my wife. I willnae abide lies between us."

"I would never lie about something so important. In the future, the Campbell Earls of Argyll take possession of Mingary Castle and my MacIan clan scatter. Many sailed for the other side of the world after hearing there would be free land. They wished for a fresh start and took it. I'm sorry I didn't tell you the truth in the beginning, but I couldn't. You hate all things MacIan."

"I detest lies more." He paced the cave's opening as he stared toward Mingary. A tic beat rapidly in his jaw.

"I'm sorry. I didn't have a choice."

"We all have choices and you've deceived me. I would never wed one of the enemy." A haunted looked clouded his eyes. "You should never have withheld this from me afore we spoke our vows."

"At the time I was a little distracted. I didn't know you were going to do that."

"Damn it." He thumped his chest. "What game does John MacIan play to send one of his own women into the enemy's camp? Can he no' fight with honor on the battlefield?"

"My being here has nothing to do with John MacIan. I wished to find Nanna, not get embroiled in a feud." She needed to touch him, to soothe the hurt she'd inflicted, but instead she kept her place. "If you wish to renounce your vow, then do it. I'd never hold you to any of the promises you made to me."

"Unlike MacIan, I hold honor, and my word remains firm." His gaze hardened. "'Tis a shame though your trust didnae come sooner." He stormed along the ledge, jumped onto the beach and snagged his black stallion's reins.

The brisk Highland wind rushed at her, flicking her hair across her face. Below, the turbulent waters surged and she pulled Calum's plaid tighter. In his eyes, she was a MacIan, and now the woman who'd deceived him.

"Calum," she yelled across the distance separating them. "I love you, but honor goes both ways. Don't let yours stand in the way of what you truly desire."

"You know what I truly desire, to ensure Duart does no' fall to a MacIan." He cinched the saddle.

Yes, she did and not for him not to have wed a MacIan. Clutching her charm to her chest, she wished with all her heart as she had that first time at Mingary. "I wish to find Nanna, safe and well. I wish to find—" The ground shook.

"Lila!" Calum shot her a look.

A massive wave rolled in and drenched her. She slipped, made a grab for the cliff but only managed air. She plummeted toward the sea. "Calum!"

Contact with the frigid water stole her breath. She kicked but her skirts dragged her down. The crashing waves tossed her about. So deep.

The plaid tore at her neck. She wrenched the pin free and the tartan jerked away in the murky waters.

What had she been thinking to stand so close to the edge? Her back slammed into the cliff and knocked the breath from her. Black hazed her vision. No. She shoved away and clawed toward the surface. She wouldn't let the sea take her, not when she was this close to Mingary. All she had to do was cross the damn sound. A mile, maybe two.

The twisting current made her lose her direction. She had to get—

A slick-skinned dolphin butted her arm, and relief burst through her. Yes. She grabbed its fin and held on tight. With one flap of its tail, it shot off, whizzing her toward the blue skies above.

Clean air washed over her face. Calum. She twisted around but the cliffs and bay were gone. Nothing appeared as it should.

The dolphin let out a squeal and she clung to it as her heavy skirts streamed behind her. The beautiful creature rounded the tip then circled one very familiar looking boulder. Her charm heated in her fist. Goodness, her wish had brought her back to Mingary. Or was it the dolphin?

The dolphin dived and she let go. She shoved her coin into her pocket then kicked for the rocky beach a hundred feet away. The cresting waves rolled her into shore.

At knee depth, she heaved her hem to her knees and traipsed out.

Mingary stood tall and strong, the castle's gray stones now a stunning pinkish-white, as it had been centuries before. Wooden outbuildings were scattered around the outer courtyard, and a horse and rider galloped along the moors toward the stables. A lad ran out of the corral to take the reins as the warrior leaped to the ground. The home of her clan, the most wondrous sight.

A call rang out from a guardsman atop the battlements. An answering shout boomed from two warriors standing on the sea-gate's stone landing. Her heartbeat pounded as one of the men withdrew his claymore from the sheath across his back.

Her arrival was unexpected, but hopefully not unwanted. She pushed her bedraggled hair over her shoulders and straightened as the armed warrior stormed toward her.

Wearing thickly furred boots and a shaggy vest over his tunic, he slapped the flat of his blade against his palm. "Who are you, and how did you sneak past the sentry guard?"

"I—I didn't see a guard. I lost my footing on the rocks around the tip and slipped into the loch. My name's Lila. I'm looking for my grandmother, Jean MacIan. She has the same silver eyes as me and I was told she'd come to Mingary."

He gripped her chin, tipped her head back. "Aye, you've the same eyes as our laird's mother, and speak as strangely too, like a Lowlander. Mistress MacIan arrived a few weeks past."

"Please, can you take me to her?" Nanna wasn't the laird's mother.

"Aye, come and warm yourself inside. I'm Ian, the laird's captain." He holstered his weapon, clasped her elbow and marched her across the beach and up the grassy incline.

Puffing, she barely kept up with her wet skirts slapping her legs.

A rock-cut ditch, close to twenty-five feet wide, curved around the castle and butted into the forty foot sheer rock wall Mingary was built on. A thick wooden drawbridge spanned the divide on the landward side. They passed under a raised portcullis, and ahead, Mingary's impregnable castle walls rose.

Through the darkened doorway, Ian steered her. "Where exactly do you hail from, lass?"

"Sydney. I lived with my grandmother there until recently." Best to keep as close to the truth as possible. Hopefully Nanna hadn't gone too far off base, even though she'd apparently claimed she was the laird's mother.

"Mistress Jean spoke of a village named Sydney when she first arrived."

"Really?" She stumbled on a jutting floor stone but quickly righted herself. A stream of light from the inner courtyard flared into the gloomy passageway and struck the corner stones. An image flittered through her mind, one of a woman standing near an ivy-covered well. The same vision from when she'd first arrived here with Zayn and wandered through the ruins. Only now the woman's face was clear. Nanna.

Clutching her soggy skirts, she raced into the courtyard. The muddy rubble littering the ground was gone and moss no longer grew in clumps along the crumbling sections of wall. Nanna stood there, her black hair wisped with gray, pinned high atop her head. Gone were the casual slacks and floral blouses she'd always adored, and instead she wore an elegant olive gown with long sleeves hemmed in layers of lace. "Is it truly you?"

"Yes, my dear. We're finally together again." Nanna opened her arms.

She bounded into them, held her tight. "I've missed you, so much."

"And I've been waiting forever for you to arrive."

"You're here. You're really here." She squeezed her and tears streamed down and mingled on their mashed cheeks.

"Look at you. You're a wet mess."

"I took an unexpected dip."

"I'm not surprised, and that sounds like a story I need to hear." Nanna glanced at Ian as he watched them from the entrance. She lowered her voice, whispering in her ear, "I haven't spoken of what's happened to us, not with John still away."

"Ian just told me you're the laird's mother?"

"Yes, I have far too much to explain, but not with an audience. Once we're alone. I promise you'll hear it all." Nanna steered her toward the winding stairs, then slowed as a maid walked toward them. "Meg, please prepare a bath for my granddaughter, and be as quick as you can. She's to have the chamber next to mine."

"Yes, my lady." The girl dashed upstairs.

Scrubbing his thickly bearded jaw, Ian stepped in front of them and barred their way. "With the laird away, I'm responsible for this clan."

"Of course you are." Nanna wrapped an arm around Lila's waist. "Thank you for bringing my granddaughter to me."

"You've never spoken of her. Isnae John your only son?"

"Yes, though he's unaware Lila lives and I wasn't certain she'd find her way here. As I told you when I arrived, I shall speak to John when he returns from the king's business in

Edinburgh. It's only right he be the first to hear my news."

Gosh, Nanna was talking as if she really was John MacIan's mother. That surely wasn't possible.

Nanna tightened her hold on her. "It'll be all right. Not long now." To Ian, she said, "Let us pass."

"Aye, you may go." He stepped aside. "We shall speak on the morrow."

Nanna guided her upstairs and along the dimly lit passageway. Ahead, two lanky lads with their shirttails fluttering loose over their breeches heaved a tub through a doorway. Nanna pressed one finger against her lips in a quiet plea to wait.

She could be patient.

They entered the chamber and the lads shuffled out. Across the room, Meg knelt at the hearth, coaxing the sparks of a welcoming fire into life. She added a log and it crackled and caught alight.

Rising, she dusted her hands against her aproned sides. "Is there aught more you need, my lady?"

Nanna smiled at her. "Yes. Could you fetch some gowns from my ambry? My granddaughter arrived without her trunks."

Meg bobbed her head and quietly closed the door behind her.

Nanna hauled her into her arms. "Finally we can talk. Tell me everything that's happened."

"I think you have some serious explaining to do first. The Laird of Mingary surely can't be your son."

"Yes, he is. I'm sorry, Lila, but I had my reasons for never speaking of who your true parents were. Time travel is in a realm all unto itself, and you were just a baby when we were first pulled through a portal into the future. I feared speaking of what had occurred because a woman would be called a witch and burnt at the stake for such talk. I had to protect us both, at all costs."

Holy moly, Nanna really was the laird's mother. A hundred

questions tumbled through her mind. Swaying, she gripped the wall. "Tell me everything."

"Honey, you were born in this time, to John's first wife who passed away in childbirth. Marybelle had a difficult pregnancy and I've always told you the truth about that. Just not what year that actually happened."

"Or exactly where." Her legs wobbled and Nanna hauled out a chair from the side table and eased her into it. She grasped Nanna's hand, needing to keep her close as conflicting emotions tumbled inside her. Had she been in Nanna's position, she'd want to protect any child in her care too, but would she have made the same decision and withheld that information for twenty-one years? Nanna certainly must have been scared. She'd traveled through time, and with a premature baby. That couldn't have been easy. Sydney too was a bustling city, and nothing like Nanna would've ever experienced here. She must have been terrified, so lost and unsure. "I'm so sorry you had to go through all of that alone. If only you'd told me."

"I adapted to the future, and to the country we'd arrived in. I would have preferred to return to Scotland, but I didn't have the means nor could I move you from your specialized care. I was without a birth certificate or passport, and I had to claim refugee status. In those first few years, I formed friendships and accepted aid where I could. I was most grateful to have a roof over our heads and food on the table. I even attended evening classes and learnt to speak without the brogue. By the time you were at preschool, I'd finally secured a job and no longer needed any benefits."

"You should have said something once I was old enough. I'm sure I would have listened." She dragged in a steadying breath. "Is John MacIan really my father? He never perished at sea?" She needed to hear it again.

"He's really your father. Before your birth, he sailed to Skye to aid our MacDonald kin. He didn't care to leave

Marybelle, but I promised him I'd look after her. Soon after he left, Marybelle began bleeding, and then her labor pains started and the healer could do nothing to stop them. After two grueling days, she gave birth to you then slipped away from us. You were more than two months premature, and so small I was able to hold you in palms of my hands. I knew death would come for you too, and my heart broke. I fell to my knees, desperate not to lose you as well. With all my heart and soul, I pleaded and wished for you to live."

"That's what started it? A wish?" She rubbed Nanna's shaky hands. "No more secrets now. We share everything."

"Yes, and my cries were heard and a portal opened." She hooked her gold necklace out from under the silk edging of her bodice. The engraved disk held the image of the unicorn as Margaret's did. "Margaret and I spoke of this, and I told you the tales as a child. There truly is folklore surrounding those born under a falling star, that they hold strong magic in their blood. That magic though will only rise when their desperation is great. With your silver eyes, you too were born under a falling star, and that night when I made my wish your eyes sparkled, as if you too understood the need to live. Then everything darkened and stars burst around us. We were transported to Sydney's hospital where technology abounded and babies born as early as you were could be saved. You lived because of my wish, and I would never take that back."

"A desperate wish to find you returned me to the past too." She gripped the charm in her pocket and it heated and calmed her racing heartbeat. "Calum has one of these charms as well, gifted to him by a fortuneteller. In your note you said it was a MacIan heirloom from the 1500s."

"I'll explain everything. I told Margaret the bare minimum, and only what she needed to know for me to ensure her trust. After I flew into Edinburgh from Sydney, the strangest sensations began to batter me. I felt driven to visit the markets, to have a reading done. When I walked into the fortuneteller's stall, she looked at me as if she'd been awaiting my arrival. She said she'd been here in the woods the night of your birth and felt the disruption in time. She'd traveled from the past the moment she was certain I'd returned to Scotland's soil. Her magic is far greater than anything I've ever seen, and the wish I'd made was nothing compared to what she'd done. She gave me your coin and told me to send it to you with the instruction to never let it go. She said she'd also traveled through time to see Calum and given him his charm. Both coins were linked, through time and their true holders' souls."

"I've felt the depth of my bond with Calum." She squeezed Nanna's hand. "Carry on."

"She said it was time for your return, and that the past must be set to rights. She told me to make a wish, but not to tamper with what she'd set in motion. Your wish had to be spoken from deep within you when your desperation was at its greatest. I couldn't tell you of her foretelling. That night I returned to my room, I made a wish, just as I'd done that first time."

"That's how you arrived at Duart?"

"Yes, but I didn't understand why I'd arrived at the MacLean stronghold until after I met Calum. He was the grounding link between us and our travel, except I couldn't tell him of what had occurred either, or stay, not when I was a MacIan. I was so worried I would be found out. Confiding in Margaret gave me the means to ensure you'd know where I'd gone to. She aided me in leaving, as she promised she'd aid you."

"She did. What happened after you arrived here?"

"There were many clan members who recognized me from the time before I disappeared. They welcomed me home, but were beyond curious about where I'd been. Twenty-one years without any word is a very long time, but I kept it simple, explaining I'd traveled to the village of Sydney where my

Cunningham kin resided, and that in all these years I'd not been able to return. Being the laird's mother, none have gainsaid my decision to speak to John first."

"I can't believe I have a father."

"Believe it." She sat on the chair beside her. "Except there is still much to be done. Your future must be fully realigned before all can be set right. You and Calum will aid each other. He is the one you're bound to."

"You mean it's not set right by my arrival here?"

"No. You're still soul bound to Calum, and if you look deep within your heart, you know he will come for you."

"Since the first time we met, we've had visions. We handfasted last night, Nanna."

"The two of you are wed?" She patted her chest. "I expected it, but that was fast."

"I couldn't deny him, and I wanted to be bound to him in the same way. Except we argued this morning. I told him who I truly was, and he was furious. He told me I'd deceived him. That was when I made another desperate wish to find you." She clasped her charm against her heart, needing its solid presence to calm her. An image of Calum crystalized in her mind and the ferocity of his grief pummeled her. Searching, he dove deep within the murky waters of the bay.

"Relax. You're here now. You've returned to Mingary and me." Nanna wrapped an arm around her shoulders, enveloping her in her wonderful lavender scent. "The one thing I've learnt in all these years is anything's possible. One simply has to look inside their heart for direction."

"I miss him, even though I wished to leave him and find you. He's loyal and honorable. Except he never wished to wed one of his enemy."

"Is that what your heart tells you?"

"Nanna, I'm not only a MacIan, but his arch enemy's daughter."

"Yes, but not all is lost." Nanna tucked a length of her drying hair behind her ear. "I'll aid you as I can, but for now we must await your father's return. Even I've not seen him, and I long for it."

"You said below-stairs he was about the king's business in Edinburgh."

"Yes, and he should have returned by now, but recently we received word of Donald and Angus MacDonald's capture. The king called John as a witness to the feud, and he can't leave until he's permitted to."

"Can we travel to him?"

"A strong escort would be needed, and that's not possible while Ian needs his warriors here to defend Mingary. We have to remain."

A knock sounded and Nanna rose and bid the servants to enter. Two maids and two lads hustled forward, each carrying a steaming pail of water. Another lass carried a tray and set it on the side table, while Meg crossed to the burgundy curtained ambry and hung two gowns.

Nanna oversaw the filling of the tub then added a few drops of scented oil and a sprinkle of dried petals.

Lila wandered toward the large bed and fingered the rich blue velvet canopy sweeping down the four-poster and onto the polished wooden floors. This was her true time. She'd been born in the past, yet never lived in it. Shocking, yet amazing.

"That's perfect." Nanna clapped her hands. "Thank you, everyone. You may all leave." She shut the door behind them. "Come, Lila. There's a warm meal. You must be hungry."

"Starving, and rather water logged, but I still can't wait to get into that bath." She sat and poked her nose into the steam wafting from the bowl of chunky seafood stew. "This smells delicious." She nabbed a slice of crusty bread, dipped it, and took a hearty bite. Warmth raced to her belly. "Could you tell me more about this feud John's gone to give his account of? I've heard Calum and Margaret's views of it."

"Of course. King James attempts to bring order, and the chiefs continue to hold onto the old ways. They have no desire to give up what is rightfully theirs. I'm afraid this time we've arrived in is one of great unrest."

"Do you know what happens? Particularly to John?"

"No. When we first arrived in Sydney, information wasn't as readily available, and even when technology advanced and more history came online, only the most remarkable accounts were recorded. John was rarely mentioned, except for the massacre following his nuptials. There is certainly nothing to say how his personal fight with MacLean ended." She knelt before the tub and swirled her hand through the water. "This is the perfect temperature. Come and have your bath."

"Calum expects an attack to come from our MacIan clan soon." She shed her damp gown, draped it over the back of the wooden chair and sank into the glorious water. "Though he's not aware John has traveled to Edinburgh, or if he is, he certainly never said anything to me."

"It's not John's intention to attack, but to ensure our defenses remain strong along our coastline. Those are the instructions he left with Ian. This past week further aid has arrived from Angus MacDonald's second, and a call-to-arms not long before that saw a dozen men arrive from Kilchoan. More calls will be made until Ian is satisfied we have a large enough defensive force." Nanna passed her the soap.

"Calum will think the clan ready for war." She lathered the soap then worked the vanilla scented suds gently through her matted hair.

"That he might." Nanna raised her hands towards the warmth of the fire. "Tell me more about Calum. I only spoke to him once or twice."

She rubbed her chest. "It feels as if I hold a piece of him locked away inside me."

"Yours is a match which shouldn't be denied."

"Bound or not, how can what Calum and I have ever survive this time?"

"Time is a fickle thing, but we are not. If there is a way, you'll find it, and I shall help you. All must be set to rights."

"Thank you for saving me, Nanna." Sloshing water, she leaned against the edge of the tub. "The wish you made the night of my birth gave me life."

"I love you too." She knelt and hugged her, uncaring she got wet. "But one day you shall spread your wings and fly. That's how things are meant to be, and even though you are John MacIan's daughter, Calum is still yours."

"Yes, he's mine." She knew it to the depths of her soul.

* * * *

Drenched, Calum paced the thin cliff ledge hours later as night fell. Since Lila had fallen into the loch, he'd done naught but search the waters and coastline. He strode to the beach, the ache in his chest so deep and unforgiving.

She belonged with him, and he'd been rash to fight with her. MacIan or not, she was his wife, and he should have listened to her concerns. He'd never make that mistake again.

White-capped waves rolled in and Colin emerged, slogging through the surf toward him. His brother had tracked him down, though he'd only arrived an hour past.

"'Tis too dark to continue." Colin clasped his shoulder. "I cannae see a thing, and with so many hours passing, it does no' look good."

"Aye, but I willnae believe her dead. She lives. I feel it." He touched his heart. "She is mine and I'll never let her go."

"Magic brought her here, and magic has clearly taken her away again."

"I was instructed to keep her safe from the sea." Calum opened his clenched fist and rubbed his charm. It had drawn blood from his tight hold. "I failed her, but I willnae again. I ride for Tobermory at first light."

"Then I'll ride with you. Arthur watches Duart. He'll ensure all is well."

"Ardnamurchan was her destination, and if a wish took her from me, then that's where she'll be. We'll search the coastal villages. I willnae rest until I find her."

"And I'll guard your back." Colin gripped Calum's forearms in a firm hold. "Virtue mine honor."

"By death or life, we stand firm together." He returned his brother's strong forearm hold.

Never would he be able to halt Colin from joining him. He would need his brother's strong sword-arm and steadying presence if he were to find his wife and bring her home.

Lila was his heart and soul, and peace would only come once he had her back.

Chapter 7

Lila scrubbed her gritty eyes then stretched and pushed her hands out from under the warmth of her bed covers. A new day dawned after another restless night spent with Calum infiltrating her dreams. The past fortnight, she'd had visions of him, and his frustration and worry had plagued her. Their bond had deepened over the past weeks, their separation not making an ounce of difference.

The door creaked open and Nanna peered in. "Good. You're awake."

"Come in."

"The seamstress finished this gown. You should wear it today." Nanna bustled across with a mass of silvery-blue fabric in hand.

"She works tirelessly." She tossed the covers and scooted out. The seamstress was always pinning one fabric or another on her and she now had the most amazing wardrobe.

"I also bring good news." Nanna smiled and her eyes lit up.

Her heart leapt. "Is it about John?"

"Yes. A scout returned during the night with word of your father's coming arrival, and this morning the tower guardsmen sighted his traveling party on the hills. He's almost here." She passed her a pair of woolen stockings. "Put this on first."

"I thought it would never happen." Finally, she was going to meet her father. She bounced onto one foot, scrunched up the hosiery leg and shoved her toes in.

"Are you excited?" She smoothed out the silk gown then held it out.

"You know I am, but I'm not sure what kind of relationship we'll have. It certainly won't be the typical father-daughter one." She flung her ivory cotton nightrail aside, slid her arms into the gown's long sleeves and dipped her head as Nanna eased the shimmery fabric over top. The layers slithered down her body and brushed the polished floorboards. "What's expected of me? How do I address him?"

"Just be yourself and don't fret."

"He's going to have so many questions, and time travel isn't exactly all that believable."

"Yes. Our news won't be easy to hear, but he must know the truth."

"That's a great plan. I'm all for honesty." She seized her charm from the side table and pocketed it. "Have you got a plan B though?"

"Plan B is still to speak the truth."

Shouts sounded outside and Nanna grasped her navy skirts and hurried to the window.

She raced after her and gripped Nanna's shoulder.

The portcullis rose from within the stone gate, the clunky sound of its chains reverberating throughout the keep. Horses' hooves pounded then a score of riders galloped in and hauled their mounts to a stop. The warrior at the party's head bounded from his destrier in leather pants and a fur vest over a dark linen shirt. His thick brown hair sprinkled with gray was messed by the wind, and more than a week's growth of stubble covered his jaw. "Is that him?"

"Yes, he looks older, stronger but older. He's the image of

his father now. Your grandfather passed away five years before you were born. John led the clan from the age of twenty."

John turned to Ian and clapped him on the back. The two conferred, their voices lost within the excited chatter of their surrounding clan welcoming the warriors home. Then John lifted his gaze and found them. Such piercing green eyes, the color of the grassy moors.

"I don't look anything like him, not the hair, eyes or face."

"No, you look just like your mother. Marybelle had black hair and dainty facial features, as you do."

An auburn haired woman in an emerald woolen riding habit called out to John from atop her horse and he crossed and assisted her down. Once on her feet, she pulled her brown fur cloak tighter about her, warding off the chilly autumn air. Her nose and cheeks glowed pink from her vigorous ride, and her breath puffed in a fog from her mouth.

"Is that Janet Campbell, Nanna?" The MacLean chief's mother appeared around fifty, only a few years older than her father's forty-six.

"Yes. She's the one who saved John's life." Nanna clutched her hand as John escorted Janet inside. "We must go."

"Do I look all right?" She fussed with her hair.

"Don't be nervous." Nanna pinched her cheeks then hurried out the door.

She chased Nanna downstairs and into the inner courtyard. The enclosed area was abuzz with their clan, a stream of them making their way toward the great hall across the paved stones.

Ian moved in beside them, his towering form blocking what little sunshine peeked through the thick patchwork of gray clouds. "The laird awaits you both in his solar. He didnae wish your reunion to take place afore all."

"Thank you, Ian." Nanna nodded briskly at the warrior who always had his watchful eyes on them.

They entered the great hall. Trestle tables held stacked

platters of cooked meat, boiled eggs, and bread. Serving maids carried trays holding steaming bowls of oats, while the returning warriors jerked out the wooden benches and sat. Just as well, her father had opted for a private meeting. She had no desire to greet him for the first time in this crowded hall.

"Oh my, there's Josiah." Nanna patted her chest. "He must have been with your father's traveling party. He was courting me in the months before you were born."

"Which one is—" Ah, no need to ask. An older broad-shouldered warrior with a weathered face and his sword swinging from his side marched toward them, his intense gaze on Nanna.

"Well, well, so my ears were no' deceiving me. Jean MacIan has returned to Mingary." Josiah motioned toward the laird's solar at the side of the hall. "Your son willnae believe his eyes either even though he's heard the news. He's anxious. You best hurry."

"It's good to see you too, Josiah." Nanna blushed, actually blushed.

"Aye, save a dance for me later when the pipers play. We have much to celebrate this day."

Goodness, Nanna had not spilled all her secrets yet, and she'd get the rest of them out of her before this day was done.

They weaved around the room, and she brushed against a wall hanging embroidered with the MacIan clan crest.

Ahead, a warrior opened the solar door and Nanna raced through.

This was the moment they'd been waiting a fortnight for. She walked in and the guard closed the door with a gentle snick.

John paced the room, his broad back carrying the weight of a sheathed claymore.

From the corner chair, Janet shot to her feet. "John, they're here."

He spun around, his gaze wide on Nanna. "Mother, is it

truly you?"

"Yes. I've so much to tell you." She rushed across the room, her arms open.

John swung her off her feet. "As do I. Mere days after you went missing, I returned from Skye to mayhem. My men had already scoured the surrounding hills for you, but I continued to search and I came upon an old woman and her son deep in the forest, a seer."

"Then you met the fortuneteller, as did I." Nanna's eyes went wide. "Did you speak to her?"

"Aye, she insisted magic had taken you away but would one day return you. 'Twas all gibberish, or at least until she spoke of the folklores surrounding those born under a falling star, the same tales you used to speak of to me when I was a lad. I sat with her around her campfire. She said she'd felt a disruption in time. I clung to her words, because you'd vanished, and I had no other answer for your disappearance than what she spoke of. She said you lived, and one day you'd return. She told me I'd have to be patient, and that your return would only occur when the time was right." He set her back on her feet. "I didnae care for that part of her prophecy, and I never believed 'twould take over twenty years for it to come about. I'd almost given up hope."

Relief poured through Lila. Her father knew. The fortuneteller had paved the way for the acceptance of their return.

"I met the fortuneteller at Edinburgh's markets," her grandmother continued. "She traveled to the future to aid me. Because of her guidance, I was able to wish my way back to the past."

"Even though I was told, 'tis hard to believe you've been beyond our time." John scraped a hand along his jaw. "Tell me what happened after Marybelle passed. I must know it all, and what started the disruption."

"Lila was so tiny, and I knew her life would end as quickly

as her mother's. I couldn't lose them both, and I made a wish with all my heart for Lila to live. A black void opened, and within the blink of an eye, we were far away."

"How far through time, and to where? I was never told, no matter how much I pleaded with the fortuneteller." He cupped Nanna's cheeks.

"We arrived at a time over four-hundred years from now, where there is such medical advancement. Lila was placed within a glass-enclosed capsule and cared for by people holding the greatest of abilities. They saved her life as none here could. Certainly no amount of searching you undertook would have found us. Oh, John, you must meet your daughter." Nanna waved her forward. "This is Lila."

"Come, child." A beaming smile lit his face.

She staggered forward, grasped his hands. "I can't believe this is happening."

"I mourned no' only my wife, but my mother and child for years. I longed for both of you to return. You have your grandmother's eyes, and those of a child born under a falling star. Did you too make a wish to return?"

"Yes, I made my wish while visiting Mingary in the future."

"You were drawn to your home. Good." He kissed her cheeks. "My daughter. I have a daughter."

Nanna wiped her eyes as she cried. "I always dreamed of this moment, to see the two of you together."

"You saved my child, Mother." He held out a hand toward Janet. "I have them back."

"You do, as you've always told me you would." She rushed across, and John pulled them all together into a hug. "The fortuneteller told you the truth."

"She did."

Nanna sniffed. "Janet, for the longest time, I've wanted to thank you for what you did in saving John's life. I read of what happened on your wedding night. The terrible massacre was recorded in history."

"Oh my." Tears misted her gaze. "You truly read of the account?"

"Yes, and my heart ached at what I read."

"My son took so many of your kin's lives that eve. 'Twas an atrocity I've never forgiven Lachlan for. I'm so sorry."

"That is his burden to bear, not yours."

"As I continually tell my wife as well." John kissed the top of Janet's head then tugged on a shaft of Lila's hair. "'Tis a miracle you're alive, something I never thought I'd see, regardless of the fortuneteller's decree."

So many emotions swamped her. Relief. Disbelief. Love. A sense of belonging and excitement stole through too. This was her father, and now they were together again, as they always should have been. "I'm so glad you're home. Now we have the chance to get to know one another."

"The king wouldnae permit me to leave until he'd entered into talks with all three chiefs. I had to wait for Lachlan MacLean's arrival."

"Nanna said you had to give evidence of what you'd witnessed."

"Aye, he questioned me about it all. Now I pray the king will come to a decision, one which will go in our favor. This feud must end."

Janet rubbed her cheek against John's shoulder. "I wish for it to end too, but no' at the loss of my son's life."

"MacLean's willful nature will be his downfall. He cannae continue to ravage the isles, plundering as he does. Although for your sake, I too hope he does no' lose his life." He glanced at Nanna. "On the night we wed, Lachlan and I argued. I hadn't expected him to demand I break my ties with my MacDonald kin and fight against them. Our marriage should have been the start of a resolution to the feud, no' to inflame it further. I was sadly mistaken."

"Yet you stayed at Duart that night. Did you not expect Lachlan to retaliate when you chose to remain loyal to your MacDonald kin?"

"I didnae believe he'd be that vindictive. Now the king will have his way. I only pray MacLean's second willnae wish to battle us in his chief's stead."

"Calum is Lachlan's captain and he's a good man," Janet pressed, intervening. "John, surely you have no' forgotten 'twas Calum and his brother who restrained Lachlan on our wedding night. As of yet, Calum has no' attacked, and I dinnae believe he will."

"Aye, though I will continue to guard and defend my land against any threat," John answered her. "The king has interceded, and I hope he can bring about a resolution, but should he no' then I will ensure Mingary does no' fall to Lachlan MacLean or his men."

A round of hearty singing broke out in the great hall and John cleared his throat. "The ale is flowing. Come, no more talk of this feud. We have much to celebrate, and our clan awaits." He flung open the door and bellowed, "'Tis time for festivity. My mother and daughter have returned."

Cheers abounded, and Lila's heart ached in equal measure. Her father's acceptance had been everything she'd hoped for, yet this feud was far too real and the stakes deadly.

"We'll sort this," Nanna murmured in her ear. "For now, let's enjoy the feast. It's time for you to get to know your father as you always should have."

Yes, this was her home, her clan. She had time now, as she hadn't had before.

Chapter 8

"Load the cart with enough provisions to send to the men." Ian's booming voice filtered through the window, ringing with authority from the lower courtyard.

At least he wasn't lurking within the hallway, awaiting Lila's first step out of her chamber this morning. In the days following her father's return, he'd ordered Ian accompany her whenever she'd wandered beyond the keep. The hulking warrior was everywhere, his protection absolute. Certainly, her father's worries were legitimate considering any wish they might make in desperation could come true, but she and Nanna had returned and were done traveling through time. This was her rightful place and here she wanted to remain.

She shoved her bedcovers back, hopped across the cold polished planks then crawled onto the wooden trunk's engraved lid under the window. After flinging open the shutters, she flipped her nightrail's hem over her dangling feet to warm them against the chill.

Outside, the sun hovered on the horizon, promising some warmth to the cool autumn day. It had poured the night before, a deluge that caused the green hills to glisten with a wealth of new growth. This land was beautiful, with its lochs and bens and grassy moors.

Better still was the view toward Mull. Each day she took a stroll along the shore and the sight toward Duart brought her closer to the warrior who never left her mind.

Goodness, she missed Calum. Their night in the cave, now three weeks past, would be forever burned into her soul. If only she could see him in truth, to have the chance to tell him she'd never set out to deceive him. A fanciful wish, one she'd never make.

"We're almost there, Malcolm. Bring the loaves of bread, beans and oats from the kitchens." Ian stood with one hand braced against the wooden sides of a cart overflowing with blankets, clothing, tools, and supplies for the warriors camped east of here.

Two lanky lads dashed out from the side entrance and tucked several loaves of bread into the rear. Both had red hair and breeches three or four inches too short on their legs. Twins, and the head cook's eldest sons. She'd come to learn they were a boisterous pair.

Hmm, where was her father? He was usually in the midst of such happenings. Maybe cloistered again with his seneschal. Yesterday he'd spent the entire day examining the accounts.

During some time alone with him in the evening, she'd explained how computers worked in the future, and how specialized software programs kept a tally of it all. He'd looked at her in complete astonishment. Oh, the things she could tell him, and would. She smiled at the thought.

"Lila, it's me." Nanna knocked then walked in with a swish of her bronzed skirts. She plowed to a stop. "Oh, why aren't you dressed?"

"I'm brooding. Where's Father?"

"He left at dawn to visit two tenants to collect overdue rents. He'll be gone for a night or two. He's organized for us to travel with the men to the camp. He thought you might like to see more than Mingary's stone walls."

Would she ever, and she'd be even closer to Calum. "How long will we be away?"

"We'll stay the night and return tomorrow with Ian."

"I can't believe Father is allowing such a trip." She jumped off the trunk. "Is Janet coming?"

"No, she left with John."

"That's a shame." She and Nanna had enjoyed spending the afternoons with Janet in her solar. The stories Janet had told them about the MacLean and MacIan clans fascinated her. Janet loved both her kin, no matter the feud and the wrongs done between them. She also held hope that one day things would ease and she'd once again be able to see her family. She missed Margaret and her grandchildren.

"You'll enjoy watching the warriors train. It's a sight to behold." Nanna crossed and glanced out the window. "Oh dear, look at poor Ian. He can't stop scratching his jaw. Clearly he doesn't care for the clean-shaven feel."

"That might be my fault. I told him ladies don't really appreciate rough beards." He'd gotten a little too close during a dance one evening in the great hall, and it had been the only way to ensure he didn't get any ideas.

"I see. He's clearly taken your word as truth. I'll keep an eye on him for you." Nanna wandered to her curtained ambry and foraged through her clothing. She hauled out a deep blue riding habit and a broad-brimmed hat. "This is perfect. I'll choose a second outfit for tomorrow and ensure it goes into my bag."

"Will I get to ride?" That's something she'd yet to experience. She tugged her nightrail over her head then folded it under her pillow.

"You'll need lessons first. For today you can ride with a warrior."

"Perfect, but anyone other than Ian." She donned the white

shirt Nanna handed her, then tugged on the fitted jacket. The riding habit's skirt was long and full, cumbersome and weighty, but the extra layers would keep her warm outside. She laced her leather boots and pocketed her charm. "Will Josiah be coming along on this trip?" Nanna and the warrior had taken an endless number of walks together.

"Yes, and I shall not be telling him he has a rough beard." Nanna fanned her face. "Sixty-five and I'm allowing a man's attentions again. Whoever would have thought?"

"Me." Nanna had so much love to give.

She splashed her face with cool water, combed her hair and left it long and loose.

"I've never considered seeing anyone in all these years, not with the secrets I've held."

A knock sounded and Nanna walked to the door and opened it.

Meg dipped her head and placed a tray on the side table.

Nanna handed her the clothing for their trip and asked her to ensure it was packed in the cart.

Meg curtsied and left.

"We have porridge and oatcakes today." Nanna pulled out a chair and sat.

They'd fallen into the routine of eating breakfast together in her chamber since Lila had a terrible habit of sleeping in. She sat next to Nanna and poured their tea. The porridge warmed her belly as she ate, though she craved something far sweeter. "I miss chocolate."

"I've been longing for cream cakes for days, the ones from our local bakery with real strawberry jam inside." Nanna bit into an oatcake and scrunched her nose. "I wonder if I can ask the cook to add more honey to these?"

"I miss hot running water and showers too."

"I miss the bowling club."

"I miss getting a good night's rest. Calum won't stop

plaguing me."

"You do look rather pale." Nanna traced under Lila's eyes with her thumb. "I could ask the healer to prepare an herbed drink which might help boost your energy."

"I'd like that." Extra energy sounded wonderful. "Then I might be able to sneak away from Ian a lot quicker."

Nanna smiled and sipped her tea.

She continued to eat as Nanna watched her, and far too thoughtfully.

"My dear, one day soon you'll have to tell John about your handfast. He needs to know about Calum. You can't keep the information from him forever."

"I know, but it isn't as if he'd bless the union and wish me well."

"No, but you should give him the chance to make his own mind up about it all. Your souls are bound."

"I can't leave here, or you."

"Mount up and prepare to leave." Ian's order rumbled through the open window.

"You miss him. I can see it." Nanna brushed the crumbs from her skirts as she stood and peered out the window. "Ah, there's the score of MacIan warriors who arrived from Kilchoan this morn. The new recruits are traveling with us."

"Did Father issue another call-to-arms?"

"Yes, even though it's only to guard and defend our shores. It's a precaution. He won't allow Mingary to fall." Nanna lifted a brow. "One of the warriors is called Wolf. We had an interesting conversation out by the stables this morning, albeit a short one. Are you aware wolves are scarce in these parts, and that they're being hunted into extinction?"

"The animal? Or the man?"

"The animal of course. Come, we're out of time for further conversation. Grab your riding hat." Nanna strode out the door.

After plunking her hat on, she tied the ribbon under her chin and followed her grandmother downstairs and into the courtyard. Nanna crossed to Ian as he held a mare for her to mount.

She veered toward the warrior mounted behind Nanna. His dark hair swept his shoulders, covering the tip of a massive two-handed claymore strapped to his broad back. "Excuse me. Do you mind if I ride with—"

He spun around, his golden gaze piercing in intensity.

She stumbled back and another warrior gripped her elbow and mumbled, "Dinnae give us away, lass. The name's MacIan, Colin MacIan. Come and meet my brother, Wolf."

* * * *

Calum wanted to grab Lila, haul her onto his horse and ride like hell from the enemy's camp. For more than three weeks he'd searched for her, only to find her here at Mingary. Instead, he extended his hand for her to take and remained as calm as he could. "Do you no' wish a ride, my lady? I vow to take care of you."

"I—I—"

Colin swung her up and Calum caught her around the waist and seated her in front of him. His hands itched to drag her against him, and he barely refrained.

"Where did—how did—" She cupped his cheek then gasped and shoved her hands into her lap. "I mean, you shouldn't be here. It's too dangerous. You could lose your head."

"The name's Wolf, and I'm no' here to lose my head. I'm here to rescue my wife," he finished in a whisper.

"I can't believe you're really here."

"As I cannae believe you're here. I've scoured this countryside, and dreamed of you every night." Arms around her, he slapped his horse's reins and followed her grandmother and the other warriors under the arch and across the drawbridge. Colin remained close on his rear in the single file stream as they entered the forest.

"I've dreamed of you too."

Which did little to deter his frustration. "I spoke to your grandmother this morn at the stables."

"Yes, well, Nanna didn't mention you were the Wolf in question. You also made your position about being wed to a MacIan clear last time we spoke. Why aren't you at Duart?"

"You're my wife. I had to find you."

"And joining Mingary's warriors was the only way?"

"Apparently. Why is your grandmother here?"

"She didn't tell you?"

"Nay. We spoke only a few words. She assured me you were safe and well, but naught else."

"Then you're really not going to like hearing my news." She gripped his leather-clad legs. "I'm John MacIan's lost daughter."

"He does no' have a daughter."

"He does now. I was born to John's first wife. Nanna was holding me when my mother took her last breath, and no one here knows about my time traveling except for him and Janet."

"I dinnae understand."

"I was born in this time, only Nanna knew I wouldn't survive my birth so she made a wish that I live, and that's when it all began. We were transported to the future, to a time when it's possible for such premature babies to survive. Every so often, a bairn is born under a falling star, and their silver eyes give them away. Nanna and I were both born so." She pulled her charm from her pocket and held it in her open palm. "I've felt you close."

"I will never be far from you. You belong to me." Her words resonated deep within him. "When I was a lad of seven, I was hunting in the forest with my father when I saw a falling star. Grief overwhelmed me in that moment, as if I'd lost something dear to me. I spoke your name, not that I understood why. I recalled that memory when the fortuneteller gave me my charm."

"So much makes sense now."

"Aye, it does. Have you spoken to MacIan about our handfast?"

"No." She shoved her charm back into her pocket. "That's not a conversation I care to have, and you risk too much by coming here."

"Aye, your father knows me well."

"What of his men?"

"The MacIan warriors I've come face to face with on the battlefield didnae survive our meeting." The chilly wind whistled through the trees and he wrapped her more securely in his arms. "John should be the only one who can identify me."

"At the cave you said I deceived you."

"'Twas said in anger and I was wrong. I want my wife back."

"But MacLeans and MacIans don't mix."

"You and I do, and I willnae hear otherwise." The need to have her back in his arms had been all-consuming and 'twas only now he felt whole again. "There is none I desire more than you. I love you, Lila."

"As I love you, but even wolves should be granted their freedom, to roam where they please."

"This wolf wishes to roam for all time with his mate. That is the only freedom I seek."

Aye, never again would he lose her.

She was his.

For all time.

* * * *

Lila had to make Calum see reason. Yes, she wanted him too, but not at the expense of escalating the feud.

They trotted out of the forest and onto the sandy shore. The waters glistened, and across the sound, the sheer cliffs of Mull stood guard like a sentinel. Their cave. It was close, a mile or two away.

"Do you feel what's between us, Lila?"

"To the point of pain." She snuggled back against him, taking what she could.

"There is only pain when we are no' together."

"My father is your enemy, even though you saved his life. Trust me, a happy family dinner isn't on the agenda when you two meet, unless it's your head being served on a platter. That I won't ever allow."

"I'll no' allow it either." Calum loosened his hold on her as two warriors galloped up from the rear and passed them. "You stay within my sight at all times."

"This is my clan. I'm not at any risk around them. You though, are." Ahead, a large group of shirtless warriors trained with the bow. They aimed their arrows at a red ribbon tied around a wide trunk a hundred feet away. Each stepped forward to take his turn, their accuracy impressive as arrow after arrow lodged within the thin strip of silk. "Perhaps you should stay close to me, and I'll protect you as I can, my wolf."

He chuckled in her ear. "Aye, then we'll do it your way, as long as the outcome is the same."

Colin rode up and leaned in. "They prepare for battle, brother."

"Aye. 'Tis only a matter of time afore they attack. I'll guard Lila while you keep alert."

"Will do." Colin nudged his horse and galloped toward the makeshift corral of beams hammered between the trees along the forest's edge.

"They're not going to attack, Calum, or at least that's what I've been told."

"MacIan's warriors have chosen a spot where they're hidden from our watchmen at Tobermory. 'Tis clear what their intentions are."

"No, if you don't attempt an attack, neither will John."

"I intend to take his newfound daughter. He'll consider that a strike at his very heart.”

“Then let me talk to him first. I can’t be the reason this feud inflames.”

“Enlightening John will only ensure you’re locked away behind Mingary’s walls and far beyond my reach. I cannae take that risk. John is no’ to hear of my intention to steal you away.”

Ahead, Ian dismounted then helped Nanna down from her horse. She was out of time to continue this discussion. “We’ll talk about this later. We’re not done yet.”

“Aye, we’ll never be done, love.” Calum pulled his destrier to a halt, jumped to the ground then swung her down beside him. “I’ll escort you wherever you need to go.”

“Ian’s under Father’s orders to do that, and he’s rather good at it too.”

“Then I’ll work around those orders. He comes. Quiet.”

Ian beckoned her to him. “I’ll show you and your grandmother to your tent.”

Nanna already cut a path along the grassy forest verge toward the erected tents. “It’s all right. I can see where she’s headed. With all these warriors about, you hardly need to walk me that far.”

He scanned the area. “Aye, though should you wander beyond this camp, ensure a guardsman goes with you.” He eyed Calum, his gaze narrowed. “Join the men in training. I’ve yet to see your skills.”

“Aye, Captain.” Calum grasped his leather bag, slung it free of his saddle then led his mount toward the corral. Not a word of resistance had he offered. He was clearly trying to remain under the radar. Good. She wholeheartedly approved of that. She wanted her wolf to remain in one piece, with his hide intact, particularly when she liked that rounded rear of his.

Ian strode in the opposite direction, heading toward the warriors training in the loch and swimming toward shore.

She clutched her midnight blue skirts and hurried after

Nanna, glad for the reprieve from both of the obstinate warriors. At the tent, she heaved the thick flap to one side and ducked inside. Nanna stood near the corner pile of pelts, innocently fingering the dark brown furs. "Nanna, you have some serious explaining to do."

"Did you not enjoy the ride, my dear?" She removed her feathered bonnet and set it carefully on top of a wooden crate next to a clay lamp.

"Wolves are scarce, huh?" She planted her hands on her hips and tried for a stern look.

Nanna giggled. "How is your Wolf? I caught sight of him after your father rode out, but we didn't have nearly enough time to chat."

"So he said, and I tried to give him his freedom, but he wouldn't hear a word of it. I even told him I'm John's daughter, but he said he's still going to steal me away." She untied her brimmed hat and tossed it on top of Nanna's. "So yes, he's well, and as stubborn as ever."

"He's your mate, Lila. You should've expected him to come. I've certainly been keeping a look out for him." Nanna hooked her arm through hers. "Come, let's freshen up. There's a glorious loch not far from here, one I remember well from my youth. It'll give us time to talk."

"We'll need a guard. Ian's orders, and for that matter, the stubborn one's as well."

"See, you already have an endearing nickname for him. I doubt we'll even need to holler. Wolves can scent their prey a mile away."

"Prey is right." Still, her heart lightened as they left the tent and Calum snuck in behind them. Deep in her heart, she wanted to be with him, couldn't believe he'd come.

They traipsed into the forest and followed the leaf-strewn path. Birds twittered overhead, and bright, dappled rays beamed through the foliage and washed over them.

Calum prowled, keeping an eye out all around. He was so infuriatingly gorgeous with that studious frown. The way he walked, so agilely his leather pants clung to his powerful thighs, made the fabric mold every single delectable inch of him. It didn't help her state of mind that the tails of his loose white tunic fluttered free from under his black vest and the breeze lifted the hem and gave glimpses of his golden skin. She leaned into Nanna's ear and mumbled, "I shouldn't want him as much as I do."

"One can't help who our heart desires."

"Nanna." She squeezed her arm. "I need you to offer discouragement right now. He's a MacLean, and now he's in danger because he came after me. Tell me how wrong our match really is."

"No, and you need to stop thinking about the feud and only consider the man who risks so much to get you back. Take each moment given to you and make it count. Haven't I always taught you that?"

"Yes, which again, is very unhelpful." Could she accept what was and live in the moment? Oh, she truly wanted to.

Calum's golden gaze clashed with hers, heating her until her blood thrummed for more.

Nanna gasped. "The loch. Look, Lila."

Small, private and perfectly round, its glassy surface danced with the reflection from the towering trees encircling it. "It's beautiful. How did you know about it?"

"Your grandfather and I stopped here one night when we returned from our honeymoon. Afterward, it was our special place and we often visited." She lifted her bronzed skirts and knelt at the mossy edge. With her hands cupped, she dipped them into the clear water and sipped. "I adored its seclusion."

"Can I take a swim?" Since arriving at Mingary, she hadn't stepped foot into the water and missed it terribly.

"Of course. It'll be a little cold, but invigorating all the same."

"You'll come for a swim too, won't you?" She loosened the ties of her riding jacket, slipped it off her shoulders then laid it overtop a boulder.

"No, it's too cold for me, and I think you and Wolf need some time alone to truly talk." Nanna hugged her then waved over her shoulder as she walked away. "Enjoy your swim. I'll ask Colin to guard the incoming trail."

So far, talk hadn't gotten them far. Still, she shed her skirt and stockings and arched a brow at her wolf. "Are you coming in?"

"Nay. I too will remain on guard." Arms crossed, he stood at the edge. "Leave your shirt on. I'll keep watch while you bathe."

"First, you need to learn the little lady has a mind of her own." She shucked the white linen and smiled as he jerked his gaze away. "Now, since it's only us, if you decide to change your mind and join me, then you know where I am." She dove into the pool and almost lost her breath at the frigid impact with the water. It was beyond cold.

She broke the surface, grabbed some decent air and dove again. She needed a warm body sliding against hers to bring back the heat, and quick. Lucky for her, the perfect warrior for the job was on hand, only time to see exactly how strong-willed her wolf could truly be.

Nanna was right. She should take each moment and make it count. Kicking underwater toward the center of the pool, she remained below until her lungs were near to bursting. Surely, he'd come soo—

A hand clamped around her ankle and dragged her upward.

She broke the surface in a slew of bubbles and gulped in great breaths. "Well, about time, Mr. Wolf."

"You tempt me beyond my endurance." With the water lapping at his waist, he leaned in and kissed her, so softly, so reverently. "You also have a beautiful mole I didn't quite see as you undressed."

"Then I insist you take a good look now. You can inspect it to your heart's desire." With her fingers deep in his slick dark hair, she returned his kiss. "This is the most magical place."

"More enchanting is my wife." The clear surface rippled as he backed her toward the edge.

"You say that now, but wait until you see me get really cranky."

"I've no' already?" He swept his hands over her bottom and caressed her cheeks.

"Not by a long shot." She rocked against the hard length of his erection. "You know, you're very hard, and that's mighty impressive for how cold this water is."

"What will be more impressive is how I put it to good use." He tipped her back until her head and shoulders brushed the mossy bank. His gaze roamed over her chest. "So beautiful. Your nipples appear ripe for the tasting."

"They're the coldest of all."

"Aye, I'll warm them first, a treasure I've longed to taste again." He cupped her breasts and weighed them in his hands before easing them together. Slowly, he licked her nipple and the hot stroke of his tongue sent a bolt of heat straight to her core.

"I love that."

He grinned then swirled around the tip. "I love it far more."

"Show me." He sucked her nipple deep into his mouth and a torrent of tingles raced through her. She grabbed his shoulders and clung. "That feels sooo good."

"Every inch of your skin must be cold. 'Tis my right to keep you warm." He swept her legs apart and eased between them.

"And to think you weren't going to hop in." She traced the ridged bands of his stomach. Talk about hard muscles honed to perfection. His abs rippled as she brushed the head of his cock.

His shaft was thick and long and saluting her from the water. She fondled the tip then stroked to the root.

His big arms bunched around her. "Aye, touch me as you please."

"The same goes for you." She squirmed forward to bring them closer together. His chest hair tickled her breasts and she sighed with delight. Then he kissed her, hot and hard until he drove every ounce of cold from her body.

He broke for air, and eyes twinkling drifted lower, kissing and licking until he reached her breasts again. He rolled one nipple between his lips until she arched back. "I have other places to devour."

"Don't let me stop you." The lush moss tickled her skin. "Let's live in the moment and put our worries aside."

"Aye, and may every moment I have always be with you." He stroked her legs then lifted them over his shoulders. Water sluiced off her skin and splashed into the loch. Head bent, he kissed along her inner thighs, his breath puffing hotly. He dipped his finger along her folds then rubbed her clit.

"Please, yes please." She grabbed fistfuls of moss. "More."

"You're a brazen lass, but aye, demand as you wish." He plunged one finger deep inside then stroked, harder and faster, until he hit that sweet spot. "Look at me, Lila. I want to see to your pleasure."

"I want to see yours too." She looked into his eyes as she searched under the water and skimmed the hard length of his cock. She caressed his hot flesh then pumped him in time with how he stroked her.

He moaned, long and low, the sensual sound thrilling her. Then he spread her legs even wider, licked her flesh in the most intimate way and built her orgasm to a pinnacle. Every flick of his tongue over her clit was such exquisite torture.

"Inside me. Now," she moaned.

"As you wish." He released her legs, lifted her against him

and filled her completely.

"Oooh, I wish." She writhed as he pumped and melded their bodies together in the timeless way of lovers. Arching, she moved with each of his deeply penetrating strokes. He'd taken her over, from the inside out and she never wanted to give him up.

"Lila, I cannae hold on much longer."

"I love you, Calum." The words rushed from her as blissful spasm after spasm racked her body. He came with her, his seed shooting deep inside as she tumbled over the edge and into oblivion.

Heart and soul, she would hold onto him.

* * * *

Calum cradled Lila against him as his breathing settled and his pulse slowed. He wouldn't leave this place without her. He kissed her, claiming her mouth as he'd claimed her body. "Are you all right, lass?"

She smiled lazily. "Wolves surely do like to do more than bathe."

"Aye, and this wolf wishes to mate for far longer, but we've been gone too long as it is." He carried her out, and as much as he detested releasing her, set her on her feet. "Dress quickly."

"We still haven't talked." She tugged her linen shirt over her damp skin then shimmied into her blue skirt, covering up every delectable inch he'd rather have on display. "Nanna and I are only here for the night."

"I'll talk with Colin, but we'll be away soon, the three of us." He dragged on his clothes.

"I haven't agreed to come." She fastened the ties of her riding jacket then straightened the hem.

"John MacIan could easily identify Colin and me should he arrive. You're aware of that." He strapped on his sword and wrist daggers. "I value my life, as I value my brother's."

"He's away until tomorrow visiting tenants and collecting

rents. He isn't coming here."

"Then you may have another night with your grandmother, but that is all." He ran his fingers through her silky black hair, tidying the damp waist length locks as best as he could. "I need you, Lila."

"The fortuneteller told Nanna that my future must be fully realigned before all can be set right. What if leaving with you isn't the right thing to do?" She grasped her skirts and walked back toward camp. "I need more time to think this through."

"When a woman joins with her husband, she abides by his decisions." He stormed after her.

"This woman doesn't, and I warned you about my crankiness." She shot him a fierce frown. "Highland warriors should come with a warning. Get involved at your own peril."

He held up a low branch, and she passed underneath. He wanted to drag her right back into his arms and see rapture again cross her face, but instead he allowed her to walk from the woods and return to her grandmother. He could bend her to his will and insist she come, but he didn't care to do so. She needed to join with him because she wished for it as greatly as he did.

"Mistress Jean asked me to guard the trail." Colin emerged from behind a tree, a curious expression on his face. "What has your woman done now to make you scowl so?"

"Wait until you're wed." He paced between two trees. "There is naught more frustrating than considering your wife's feelings. She has no' had enough time with her grandmother and father."

"The warriors at camp say she's John's daughter, and their laird is well pleased with her return." Colin motioned toward the loch's tip. "I discovered three fishermen's skiffs beached beyond those rocks. Any one of them will do if we wish a quick escape."

"Then on the morrow's high tide we'll sail for Duart."

"You'll have your wife's agreement by then?"

"Aye, somehow." He'd never leave her behind.

Chapter 9

The next morning, Nanna dressed in a whirlwind, acting as nervous as any girl about to go on a date. Lila sighed contentedly as Josiah kissed her grandmother's hand then escorted her from the tent. It was wonderful to see Nanna so happy again.

Alone, Lila tidied her bed of brown fur pelts, adjusted the long lace sleeves of her golden gown and stepped outside. The air held a slight chill, but the sun shone high.

"Are you looking for your grandmother, my lady?" The matronly cook scrubbed a pot on the trestle table nearest the fire pit. "She and Josiah have just wandered down along the beach toward where the men train."

"That's all right. I'll see her later." She nabbed a folded drying cloth from the table and walked toward the other end of the camp. A ripple of awareness heated her body. Calum. He was close, his presence firing all her senses.

She turned around and almost toppled over. Good heavens. He strode toward her in black hip-hugging rawhide breeches, his tanned chest bare and displaying a healthy sheen of sweat. Her mouth watered to take a bite out of him. Why did he have to look so damn scrumptious all the time? "You need to cover up."

His gaze dropped and fastened on the low neckline of her

gown. "As do you. Did the seamstress get your measurements wrong?"

"No. I think this is the fashion. Don't you care for it?"

"I'd rather see it off you than on." He caught her elbow, guided her past a cluster of boulders and toward a natural hollow within the rolling sand dunes.

Once out of view, he motioned for her to sit, and going by the determined look in his eyes, she wasn't about to argue. She plopped down, tipped her slippers off and dug her toes into the soft sand. "How was your sleep?"

"I prefer my wife at my side than a hundred snoring men." He knelt and traced one finger along the top rise of her breasts. Her nipples beaded and scraped with aching need against the fabric barely keeping them in. "Your breasts appear sensitive."

"They are when you touch me like that." She looked into his eyes and her heartbeat raced. "That was an invitation in case you missed it, my wolf."

He chuckled, claimed her lips and kissed her. Their breath melded, and she caught his wide shoulders and scooted closer. She wanted him, badly, and she'd never be able to deny this connection. It pulsed with such strength between them.

Slowly, he skimmed her sides then stroked her hips and belly. "Colin and I will borrow one of the skiffs. We leave within the half hour."

"I didn't say I was coming."

"I know, love, but I need you to all the same." He slipped the edge of her bodice to one side, dipped his head and grazed his teeth over her nipple. "I cannae leave without you, and if I stay, my capture will only be a matter of time. You need to come."

"I—I—" She was sunk, her resolve disappearing fast. "You do not fight fair."

"Is that an aye?" He brushed his mouth over hers in a teasing caress.

She was out of choices. His safety had to come first. "Yes, I'll come, but you have to agree that Nanna can visit as often as she likes. I also have to have your assurance I can return to Mingary whenever I need to visit my father."

"Your grandmother is welcome and will be afforded safe passage to Duart's sea-gate." He fixed her bodice, covering her up. "I'm sorry. Visiting Mingary right now is out of the question."

"Then allow my father safe passage as well."

"John will never accept that invitation."

"I finally have a father. I want to get to know him."

"Once this feud calms, I'll do all I can to grant your request. I give you my word." He tugged her to her feet and kissed the top of her head. "Pack what you need and say your goodbyes to your grandmother. Colin and I will be waiting for you here."

"Hmm, I prefer it when you get all stubborn and I can argue back as I please. I'm not sure about this persuasive side of you." She turned on her heel and marched back the way she'd come. For now, she'd ensure Calum's safety then she'd worry about the rest of her issues later.

Nanna stood before their tent, a knowing smile on her face. "You appear a little flustered, my dear. Is all well?"

She ducked inside, tugging Nanna along with her. "Calum insists we leave right now."

"You're his wife. Should he be discovered, his life would be forfeit. Of course, he'll want to leave. Surely you knew his request would come."

"Loving him is so frustrating." Adjusting her tight bodice, she blew out a long, steadying breath. "Although, he did agree to your safe passage to Duart. You'll come, won't you?"

"Try to keep me away." Nanna hugged her. "I'll speak to your father. This news won't go down well with you beyond his reach at Duart, but your handfast vows give Calum the same rights as marriage vows do, even if only for a year and a day.

Don't fight what should be." Nanna released her. "Do you have your charm? The fortuneteller said you must always keep it on you."

"Yes." She patted her pocket.

"Good. Go quickly, and travel safely. I'll do all I can to hide your leaving, for as long as I can."

"I love you, Nanna." She grabbed her bag.

"I love you too, and we shall see each other soon. I'll make certain of it." Nanna poked her nose out the flap. "All is clear."

She kissed Nanna's cheek then scurried around the tent and into the thick woods. At least she'd never be more than a day's travel from her. She'd sort this all out somehow. There had to be a way.

With her nerves stretched, she weaved between the trees and came out near the sand dunes where she and Calum had spoken. Hidden by a clump of boulders on the rocky shore from those at camp, the two men held the sides of a fisherman's skiff in thigh-deep water.

Calum surged out, scooped her into his arms and strode back to the skiff. "Did you leave without any issue?"

"Yes. Nanna kept a lookout."

"Thank you for coming. I didnae care to steal you away." He leaned into the boat and settled her on the wooden bench. She didn't doubt he would have done so had she fought his decision to remain.

"Then let's get moving." She stowed her leather bag under the bench next to his. She couldn't believe she was leaving, except Nanna was right. She and Calum were destined to be together, and she loved him. He was the only man she wished to spread her wings and fly with.

"You should have fought a little harder, Lila." Colin jumped in. "I was looking forward to seeing Calum having to fetch you."

"My wife certainly knows how to spar." Calum bounded

aboard, splashing water into the hull. He grabbed his plaid from his bag and wrapped it around her. "It can be cold out on the water."

"Just get this skiff moving before someone sees us. I prefer we don't have an all-out war on the water." She wriggled one hand free and nudged him toward the bench. "Move it."

"Aye, my feisty one." He settled on the center seat, grabbed the oars and rowed toward the mouth of the loch.

Colin kept a lookout.

All remained clear, and she burrowed, bringing Calum's plaid over her nose. Entrenched within the warm wool, his fresh outdoor scent surrounded and comforted her.

"No one follows," Colin declared and gripped the ropes.

"Then we raise the sail." Calum tucked the oars away and grasped two of the ropes Colin held out to him. The wind filled the sail with a hearty slap, and with their feet braced wide along the side, the skiff shot off like an arrow. "The winds are strong. Come here, Lila."

She scrambled across and clutched Calum's waist. "Promise me you'll get us to Duart safely."

"I would never risk your life."

Their side rose out of the water, and both men leaned farther back to counter the move. She toppled against Calum until she lay half over top of him. If she reached out, she'd be able to touch the white-capped waves. The sheer power of the wind amazed her. They'd certainly cross the short mile between the isles in no time. "This is an interesting way to travel."

"There's naught like sailing the seas."

The wind whipped her hair into a frenzy and pulled the side pins free. "I've always lived near the ocean but never sailed like this. Australia is one large country. Perhaps a hundred times the size of Scotland, and we usually travel in vehicles. They're steel contraptions that roll on wheels, and they move fast."

"Australia is still across the ocean. You must have sailed

the seas to reach Scotland."

"In the future one can board a plane, a huge vessel which carries hundreds of people and flies across the sky. I traveled half way around the world in just one day."

"Unbelievable." Colin whistled, his dark hair blowing in the breeze. "What else does the future hold?"

"The greatest opportunities. Children are taught to read and write, from a very early age." She stroked Calum's broad chest as a seagull screeched overhead. "Girls and boys both."

The boat crested a huge wave, which came out of nowhere. Calum gripped the ropes tighter, his biceps bulging and every muscle straining to control the wind power harnessed in the skiff's tight sail.

"Hold tight," he bellowed.

The bow rose sharply upward.

"'Tis slippery," Colin yelled as he grappled to keep his footing.

The hull slammed down and the impact sent Colin flying.

She screamed as he disappeared within the raging waves. "No! We have to stop. Turn back, Calum."

"He can swim. Look how close we are to Mull. There's our cave." Colin's loose ropes hit the sail and pinged off with a drumming whop. Calum jerked forward to seize them.

She pitched sideways and hit the icy water. The current rolled and twisted her tartan wrapped skirts around her. Clawing, she fought to free herself.

With the tartan gone, she kicked, thrusting through the murky depths. She broke the surface and shoved her tangled hair back. The skiff had overturned and the surf crashed over the curved hull. It popped bow up then slowly sank. Gone, swallowed whole.

"Lila!" Calum's shout blasted from somewhere between her and the sunken vessel.

"Calum!" Colin's shout came from not far behind her.

They'd all escaped and survived.

"Look for Lila, Colin. She fell no' long after you."

"I'm here, and fine, Calum." Her skirts dragged, but she swam toward shore. "Race you both to the beach."

"Where are you?" Calum snapped, his shout closer, and then he was there, catching her around her waist and kicking for her. He propelled them both toward land. "I'm no' allowing you within ten feet of the water once we're back on firm soil."

Colin swam in beside them. "'Tis no wonder the fortuneteller told you to keep her safe from the sea."

The surf rolled them up onto the beach and she collapsed onto her back on the sand.

Heaving deep breaths, Calum and Colin flopped onto their backs on either side of her.

"Are you all right?" Calum caught her hand, twined their fingers together.

"There's nothing like a refreshing dip to wake one up." Birds soared above then dipped to land on the highest branches of the towering trees. She dug into her skirt pocket and clasped her charm in her chilled fingers. "At least I didn't lose this."

"I'll go build a fire to warm us up." Colin pushed to his feet and slugged toward the forest's edge. He collected driftwood along the way then in a sheltered spot near the tree line, laid his armful down and dug a hole.

The wind whistled and she shivered at the cold blast. She had to get out of her heavy gown. The linen sark she wore underneath should cover her adequately. She unlaced the stays and tried to drag her arms out of the long, clingy sleeves. "Can you help me?"

"Aye. Your gown will dry quicker if we hang it over a branch." He crouched in front, and wriggled the fabric down her hips and off.

She slid her coin into her sark's concealed front pocket. "I'm thirsty. I think I swallowed some sea water."

"We'll get you fresh water." He steered her toward the stream gurgling into the loch. "I'll watch over you."

"Thank you. The last time I drank from here didn't go so well." She knelt, dipped her cupped hands into the brook and slowly sipped.

Calum held her hair from flopping forward. Even though the water was chilly and hit her empty belly, no dizziness assailed her. Splashing her face, arms and legs, she washed away as much salt from her skin as she could. "What's the plan now since we didn't make it to Duart?"

"We'll walk to the village of Craignure and hire horses. 'Tis close." With his hands around her waist, he drew her to her feet. "Can you walk?"

"Yes. I don't think we should stay here for any longer than we need to."

"With the skiff sinking, there is little to track us with." He stroked her cheek, his hungry gaze dipping to the sagging neckline of her sark. "I want to kiss you."

"So I see." Her pebbled nipples poked the thin cloth. "Where would that be exactly?"

"Everywhere." Golden eyes twinkling, he slid his hand around the back of her head and brought her mouth to his. He kissed her, his lips scorching a hot trail across hers and leaving her breathless.

"What about Colin?"

"Damn. I lose my mind when I'm around you." He tugged his sodden tunic off then slipped it over her head. "Let's warm you first afore the fire."

"Calum!" Colin sprinted toward them. "MacIans. Crossing the sound."

A horn sounded with one long and eerie blast across the bay. A loud roar boomed from a dozen warriors on board a birlinn. At the helm, Ian bellowed an order and the men tightened the sail and changed course directly toward them. The vessel flew across the water.

"Hell, they must have seen us." Calum snatched her hand and raced her toward the nearest tree. With his hands on her hips, he boosted her into the bow where it formed a solid V. "Remain here, out of sight."

"Don't leave me." She clung to her high spot.

"No one will take you from me. I promise you." He slid his ever-present claymore free of its side scabbard. No. Surely he and Colin weren't about to battle so many warriors on their own.

"If you get hurt, I won't speak to you ever again. Remember that. No more cranky wife for you."

"I long for our next argument. I'll take the utmost care." He raced toward the loch.

If only they hadn't been seen. She couldn't lose him.

* * * *

Calum skidded in beside Colin. Beyond the breakers, a dozen warriors plunged their oars into the sea and powered their vessel in. Ian MacIan pumped his fist into the air and ordered his men to lower the sail. They slashed their oars in the reverse direction and slowed their speed.

"The guardsman at Craignure will raise the alarm. He'll no' miss their arrival." Colin gripped his sword.

"Aye, until our warriors arrive, we will fight."

Two warriors leaped into the waist-deep water, seized the bow and held the birlinn steady. MacIan bounded over the side and slogged toward them, the surf crashing into the back of his knees and spraying in a wide arc. "MacLean, you'll return my laird's daughter now."

Motioning Colin to remain at his flank, Calum stepped forward, one eye on the warriors still onboard and awaiting their captain's orders. "'Twas Duart she first came to many weeks ago. Lila and I handfasted, and afore she was aware of her parentage, or I of hers."

"You're aware now, and surely you've nay wish to remain

wed to one of us?"

"I willnae hand her over."

"Repudiate your vow. Or mayhap you prefer death to achieve the same means." He heaved his claymore free and swung his blade between him and Colin. "You two are by far outnumbered."

This oncoming battle was inevitable, and Calum's blood roared for justice, to have his wife by his side and ensure she remained safe and well. He raised his blade. "Leave, or fight. 'Tis your choice."

"Aye, an easy one to make," MacIan snorted. "Your death awaits."

"As does yours." Calum blocked MacIan's swift attack. Their weapons clashed dead center, steel ringing loud against steel. "I see you dinnae wish to hold back."

"'Tis been too long since I last battled a MacLean." MacIan came at him, landing several hard blows one after the other in an attempt to find his point of weakness. "You prefer your right arm."

"I prefer to live." He sprang forward and fought. Lila needed him alive, and there was no greater incentive than to fight for her and their future together.

From the birlinn, the MacIan warriors cheered their captain on.

"No! Stop!" Lila tore down the beach, her midnight black hair streaming behind her. "No one is allowed to die because of my stupid wishes."

"Lila, nay." Colin caught her. "Dinnae enter the battle. This is Calum's fight."

"Let me go." She thrashed against him. "Calum, behind—"

MacIan swung and Calum barely met the staggering blow. It knocked him to his knees, their blades crashing together an inch from his nose. His arms shook as he gripped his two-handed sword and tried to heave to his feet.

"You appear to be in a predicament." MacIan sniggered and shoved down harder. "Care to yield? Or do you wish for your bride to see your death?"

"The only one to die this day will be you." He swept his leg out, thumped MacIan in the shin then shot to his feet. He barely ducked MacIan's next blow, but at least he was upright and back in with a fighting chance.

"A lucky move, MacLean."

Driven, he slammed his blade into MacIan's and the warrior stumbled in the incoming tide. He knocked MacIan's weapon away, grasped his throat and thrust his knee into his belly.

"No, Calum," Lila yelled. "Don't inflame the feud."

"'Tis already inflamed." Giving MacIan his freedom wasn't an option, not when he still had a dozen warriors waiting in his wings. He pushed MacIan's head under the water and held him down.

The tide receded and MacIan grabbed a breath. "My laird will never allow his daughter to remain here on Mull." To his men he shouted, "Death afore surrender."

A roar came from the warriors. Hell. He shoved MacIan away and met the new threat.

Chapter 10

"Calum needs you." Lila struggled against Colin's hold. "Don't let him fight this battle alone."

"Promise me you'll return to the trees."

"Yes. Go."

Calum slashed his blade at one man after another, while behind him Ian seized his wrist dagger, his marked target Calum's back.

A scream tore from her throat and echoed all around.

Colin sprinted toward the loch, bellowing Calum's name.

She sped after him.

This was all her fault. Calum would die because of her.

Splashing through the water, she grabbed her pocketed charm and cried out, "Save Calum and take me home. I wish for him to live, so I might return to love him again one day."

A dolphin arched out of the water and slammed into Ian. He went sprawling head first into the foamy waves, his dirk slinging off course and embedding deep within the birlinn's side.

Desperation drove her on, and she slogged through the waves, heading for the one man who was hers.

Calum ducked the oncoming warrior's blade then speared a look toward her. "No more wishes, Lila. Get back."

"I love you, and we're in this together. I wish for a lifetime with you, in whatever way it's possible to have it." A dolphin whizzed under the water, a murky gray shadow knocking her feet from under her. She went down, water closing over her head.

She grabbed its fin and held on as the dolphin shot off. It broke the surface and peered at her with silver eyes so hauntingly like her own. They sparkled, like magic.

With a squeal and splash of its tail, it rose, flipped in the air then swam away, leaving her in the deep near a raised boulder.

Across the water, Mingary perched on a rock ridge overlooking the loch, its stone walls crumbled with the passage of time. On the shore, Zayn paced in his wetsuit, his hand raised to his brow.

A well of emotions swarmed up inside her, battering her heart and soul.

She clutched her spinning head, despair as deep as the ocean smothering her.

A wave crested and tumbled her in toward shore.

Zayn sprinted into the water, hooked an arm around her waist and helped her onto the beach. "I've been so worried. Where have you been?"

"There was an earthquake and—oh, dizzy." Her knees buckled and she fell onto the sand.

"Are you okay? You've been missing for an hour." Zayn dropped in beside her. "I lost sight of you after the dolphin ride. I didn't mean to get so carried away, but I—" Frowning, his gaze moved over her body. "Where's your wetsuit?"

"I'm wearing it." She grasped her legs, only she encountered thin ivory linen underneath a man's white shirt. "Well, I was wearing it." How had she lost her wetsuit? Her head was so cloudy, and her thoughts scattered. "I don't feel so good."

He stared into her eyes then lifted one lid. "Your eyes are glittering, so bright. I've never seen the like before, though I've heard folk stories. Every now and then, a child is born under a falling star. Their silver eyes sparkle when the magic within their blood rises."

"That sounds familiar. Nanna told me that tale as a child too."

"Something must have happened out there." Zayn lowered his hand. "You can't go from wearing a wetsuit to this kind of clothing and not know about it."

"The earthquake struck and I slid off the boulder. The waves tossed me around and then…" What had happened next? She tried to search for a memory, only nothing but a black void filled the space. "Um, there was definitely a dolphin. It came to my rescue just now. I can't explain the clothing."

"When I couldn't find you, I called Dad on my cell phone. We should get you checked out. You may have hit your head. The confusion isn't a good sign."

"Yes, that might be for the best." She pressed her charm against her chest, and relief poured through her.

"Zayn!"

A suited man in his forties raced down the grassy slope and onto the rocky beach, one finger holding his round-lensed spectacles on the bridge of his nose. Behind him, the sun dipped along the horizon.

"Dad, I found her." Zayn hoisted to his feet, clasped her hand and pulled her up beside him. "Lila's been in the water a long time. She's feeling dizzy and confused."

"Grab the bikes and load them onto the rack. I'll help Lila." He straightened his navy and white striped tie from where it had flipped over his shoulder. "Can you walk?"

"Yes." She stumbled and he caught her. "But I won't say no to a helping hand."

"Let's get you to the hospital." Zayn's father steered her toward his black SUV, opened the rear passenger door and settled her inside. He rummaged in the boot and returned with a red and blue swathe of tartan so similar in color to, well, so similar in color to someone else's. Only whose? "Wrap yourself in this."

She snuggled into its warmth while Zayn heaved the bikes onto the roof rack with a loud clunk. With her frozen fingers, she clenched her charm tight. "I'll never let it go, Nanna. I promise," she whispered to herself.

"In the car, Zayn." Mr. MacKeane jumped behind the wheel and shut his door.

Zayn hopped into the front seat, tossed their bags through the gap into the rear beside her then secured his seatbelt. He peered around his chunky headrest toward her. "You okay?"

"I'm g-good."

"Hit the gas, Dad. I've never seen anyone look so blue."

The SUV rumbled to life and they bumped along the gravel track with the headlights guiding their way. Mingary disappeared into the dark as they wound around the hills. Once they reached the end of the private road, they turned onto the blacktop and continued through the rural countryside toward Kilchoan. Her heart ached with each mile they traveled away from Mingary, and as she squeezed her eyes shut, tears escaped and flowed down her cheeks. She was never this emotional. She really must have hit her head, because she'd never experienced this level of confusion before.

Out the window, the moon hung like a fiery orange ball, bathing its shimmery golden hue over the fields of green. Smoke curled from the chimney of a sprawling wooden-shingled home then vanished on the wind. Like time itself, there one moment and gone the next.

"You're not talking much." Zayn squeezed her leg.

"N-not much to say." Her teeth chattered fiercely.

He knocked his father's arm. "Hurry it up, Dad."

"She'll be in shock, Zayn. Keep an eye on her. I'm driving as fast as I can."

They drove into the village and sped along a side road running parallel to the main street. Ahead, a single story hospital with a glass entrance wavered before her eyes.

Zayn's father zipped into the first parking space. "Help Lila in while I let them know she's coming."

"I'm on it." Zayn whipped open her door, slung an arm around her waist and hauled her out. "Lean on me."

"I—I—" Her vision blackened and her head shattered with pain. She slipped sideways and into oblivion.

* * * *

Calum bumped into something as he pushed through the murky depths of the loch. He tried to grab hold of it, only he got nothing but water. Damn, he was almost out of breath. He kicked upward, broke the surface and treaded. He'd returned from Skye this eve with Colin and still had the fortuneteller's prophecy humming through his mind. No one could disappear into thin air, but that old woman had after handing him a charm.

Now he was swimming in the loch for no good reason.

The stars twinkled in the dusky evening sky, a glittering ribbon shining over Duart's massive fortified walls. The guardsmen on watch patrolled the battlements, keeping an eye out for any possible attack. 'Twas only a matter of time before MacIan sought his revenge for the atrocity done to him and his clan, and Duart was his to protect.

He kicked toward land, made the beach and collected his tartan and sword. His vision hazed and images flickered through his mind, a wispy barrage until just one became staggeringly clear. A woman. She turned toward him, her body covered in sleek, black fabric glistening from the water. Midnight-black hair streamed to her waist, and her enchanting silver eyes sparkled.

The image dissolved and his heart ached with loss.

Hell, he was losing his mind.

He strode into the keep, signaled the guard to lower the portcullis then walked up the tower's side stairs. Once in his chamber, he shut the door and stoked the fire to blazing life.

"This is amazing."

He spun around and a woman's image flickered to life.

She wandered toward his side table. She picked up the pitcher, poured water into the basin then traced along the rim. "What a beautiful antique."

"'Twas gifted to me, but 'tis no antique," he answered her.

"Oh, sorry. It looks like one." She drifted to his desk, inspected his candleholder then glanced at the ceiling.

"Who are you?" He wanted to touch her, hold her, feel the warmth of her skin against his.

"You know who I am." She crossed to his bed and stroked the fur covers. "I'm your charm. For all time. I'll come back to you. I promise."

Her image wavered and disappeared.

His loss intensified.

* * * *

"Would you care for a fresh glass of water with your medication?" An auburn-haired nurse buzzed around Lila's bed, tucked in her crisp white sheets and smoothed the blue woolen blanket.

"No, the one I have is fine. How far away is the doctor?" She was desperate to leave after suffering through three long days of observation by the medical team. Blacking out had not been fun, nor when she'd finally awoken, being told she wasn't going anywhere. She didn't have time to laze about when she had Nanna to search for.

Mingary hadn't turned up anything during her trip, but the next location on Nanna's itinerary was Duart. The urge to get there was the strongest she'd ever had.

"Dr. Cardiff is doing her rounds. I'll let her know you're waiting."

Her matronly doctor strode in, her shoes clipping loudly on the linoleum floor. "I heard my name."

"You did. Lila wanted to see you." The nurse walked out with a cheery smile.

"I have your test results." The doctor flipped her white coattails and perched on the bed beside her. "Your blood work shows you're pregnant."

"I'm what?"

"You're pregnant."

"Are you sure?" The doctor must be mistaken. One couldn't get pregnant when one hadn't had sex.

"Yes, the results were conclusive."

An image flittered into her mind, one of a blazing fire, the shadow of its flickering flames grazing the stony walls of a cave. Heat pulsed through her body, and a man with dark hair and golden eyes released the plaid still covering her until the soft wool pooled in her lap.

"Calum, show me everything you saw in your vision." The words were her own, spoken to him. She loved him and the emotion consumed her with its intensity.

"Aye, everything." With painstaking slowness, he grazed a finger from between her breasts to her belly, his touch starting a pulse point fluttering between her legs.

"I really like how you touch me."

"I like it more." He skimmed his hands over her waist and pressed his lips to her belly. He kissed her, right over her heart shaped mole. "Beautiful, and just as I saw it."

"How about you show me your star shaped birthmark?" She tickled down his side and around to his right cheek. "It was about here, wasn't it?"

"Aye, though I intend a long loving of your body first." He laid her back on his plaid, eased her breasts together and licked one nipple.

"I never want to forget this night."

"I'll ensure it." He swirled around the tip then sucked her nipple deep into his mouth. She pushed her hips against him.

He'd awakened her body, and she wanted more. She craved his—

"Lila?" The doctor nudged her. "Are you all right?"

"Yes."

She was pregnant, by a warrior named Calum.

Her heart ached for him.

"I can release you as soon as you're ready now we're aware you're healthy and well." The doctor slid her chart from the rail at the end of her bed and wrote on it.

"Thank you. I need to leave."

"Then I wish you well with your pregnancy. Take this to reception." She folded the paper, passed it to her and left.

Wishes, yes wishes.

More memories assailed her.

Calum set his hands on her hips and slowly, carefully, moved between her legs. He nudged his cock along her slick folds. "Do you trust me?"

"Yes, hurry. I'm burning up for your touch."

He kissed her then pushed against the barrier, tore through and plunged inside. They were joined so deeply. "We're one, and none shall ever tear us apart. You're my charm," he whispered. "There is no escaping me now."

Calum waited for her, and she wanted the real man, not memories. She had to find him.

She thrust the bedcovers away, grabbed a pair of slim black jeans from her bag that Zayn and his father had brought from her hotel and wriggled into them. She slipped her favorite white t-shirt over her head, shoved on a pair of leather sandals and nabbed her brass charm.

With her bag in hand, she marched to the front desk and paid her bill.

Outside, she caught a cab and asked the driver to take her to the ferry terminal. She'd bypass Mingary and go straight to Duart Castle. That was where he'd be. She was certain of it.

Once onboard the sleek, white-paneled ferry, she darted around the passengers and at the bow, gripped the polished wooden handrail. Above, heavy gray clouds swept the sky.

As they cruised down the sound, they passed the sheer cliffs of Mull and hers and Calum's bay. Their cave was half hidden by scraggly bushes, but it was still there. How could she have forgotten him?

They made berth at Craignure, the small settlement no longer hidden beyond the trees, but nestled right up to the water's edge. Seagulls circled the fishermen's boats and water sloshed against the thick round wharf pilings as they moored.

She hurried toward a tour coach as the driver made his last call for passengers to Duart. With her ticket paid, she sat and clutched her charm during the short drive.

Duart appeared, standing high on the rise of a craggy hill, the moors a lush green surrounding it. The castle appeared larger than life, and canons now graced the front grassy area, pointing toward the loch, relics concreted in place from an era long gone.

She disembarked, paid her entrance fee at the booth and dashed inside.

Every moment they'd spent together returned to her. He was hers, and their souls were bound.

Inside the great hall, heat pulsed from the lit fireplace. The flames shot up the stone flue and sent a wash of golden light across the MacLean clan's silver shield strung above it. It was still here as it had been in the past.

The castle's uniformed guide called everyone to gather closer, but she snuck up the winding stairs to the second floor. The gleaming dark wood of Calum's door beckoned, and she grasped the brass knob and shoved it open.

A chill hung in the air, and a draft swept in where the window remained an inch open. She ducked under the roped off portion and moved toward Calum's side table. It still held a pitcher and basin, the beautiful set unchipped although not the one gifted to him.

She drifted to his bed, rolled onto it and caressed the soft brown fur.

"I love you, Calum. I'm sorry I left you. If there was any other way to have remained with you, I would have taken it." She pressed her charm to her chest and her heartbeat pulsed against her palm. All went eerily quiet. "I wish, with all my heart, to find a way back to the man my soul cries out for. Please return me to Calum."

Out the window, thunder boomed and blackened clouds rolled in. A mist rose from below, and from one second to the next, surrounded her. She scrambled to the end of the bed, but only a black void appeared below. The wind swirled and a dark force sent her sprawling into the murky abyss.

Terrified, she screamed.

Then slammed into a wall of water.

She kicked and fought the churning current, her lungs burning for air.

* * * *

Pacing the castle's battlements, Calum clasped his charm. Three days had passed since the fortuneteller had left and he'd seen the woman's image in a vision. She haunted him, as if a ghost from his past. Why couldn't he remember her?

At least Colin was due to return on the morrow from Tobermory. He'd seek his counsel.

The moon's glow cast a silvery hue over the stillness of the loch, with not even the slightest breeze to draw a ripple.

The earth shook and he gripped the thick stone crenellation. Thrice this day the ground had moved so.

Starlight flashed off the water in a blazing display.

Hell. He had to get down to the loch. Now.

Everything within him demanded it.

Sprinting, he took the stone steps four at a time and raced out the entrance. At the water's edge, he shucked his boots then searched again for the lights. More concentrated now, they churned within a swirling vortex. He dove in and swam into the heart of it.

It sucked him down, an unearthly force he'd never fight.

Chapter 11

With a tight grasp on her charm, Lila fought the icy water as a blaze of lights shimmered all around. It was as if the stars themselves had escaped the sky. Beautiful, yet deadly. She had to get—

An arm clamped around her waist.

She jerked around and stared into the most piercing golden eyes. Calum firmed his hold on her and pushed them upward through the murky depths, and in a flurry of bubbles, they broke the surface.

She gulped in great drafts of air. "I-is it really you? Or have I died and gone to heaven?"

"Who are you? Why have I been longing for your arrival?" He cupped the back of her head and drew her closer. His dark hair floated around his neck as he treaded water for them both.

"I came as soon as I could." Her Highlander was real, his body solid, his flesh warm and his hold tight. She clutched his shirtfront as the lights around them blinked out. "Don't you remember me?"

"I've seen a vision, and three days past, a fortuneteller spoke of you."

"I'm Lila." She'd returned to the same time she'd first

arrived. "I'll help you remember, but this water's cold. Do you mind taking me inside?"

"Aye, I must warm you up." He kicked them toward the shore, swept her into his arms and carried her out. Water sluiced from their bodies, and she shoved her coin into her pocket as Calum's gaze roamed her body. "What are these clothes you wear?"

"Jeans, and they'll be tough to get off now they're wet."

"I'm sure I'll manage, ah—" He shook his head. "My apologies. I didnae mean to be so forward."

She stroked his cheek. "Take me inside, and you can be as forward as you like."

He hurried, bounding up the winding stairs and into his chamber. He shut his door then motioned toward his trunk where a tartan was folded on top. "Use what you'd like. Wrap yourself up."

"From memory, you're very good at warming me up all on your own." Nothing would heat her blood faster than his touch, and she longed for it, to the depths of her soul.

"I dinnae—" He grasped the edge of the table and closed his eyes. "A vision."

"Tell me about it."

He moaned as if in pain. "You have a beautiful heart shaped mole on your belly."

"What else do you see?"

With his eyes still closed, he murmured, "You lie afore me in a darkened cave. Your beautiful hair is spread like black silk over my tartan, and your body is entwined with mine. No part of us remains apart."

"Keep watching." She stroked his back as he did.

"We're speaking vows and—" He slowly straightened and turned around. Desire blazed in his eyes. "You're my wife?"

"Now we're getting somewhere." She tugged her cotton t-shirt free then tossed it onto the polished floor where it hit with a resounding slap. "Now, show me exactly how we fit together."

"Are you"—his devouring gaze lowered to her chest—"certain?"

"Touch me, Calum. I want you to remember everything as I have."

He embraced her breasts and nuzzled between them, his mouth moving hot and swiftly over her flesh. "I recall making love to you in a hidden loch. Your breasts are so beautiful. So full."

"Yet still a little cold."

"Sorry, my love." He drew her nipple deep into his mouth and sucked, hard.

"Mmm, much better. You are so good at that."

"We crossed the sound but sunk the skiff," he murmured. "There was a battle and you disappeared within the waves. I remember. You wished yourself away from me." He lowered to his knees, planted his hands on her waist and trailed his lips down. He kissed her, right there where their child lay. "Where have you been?"

"A medical facility in the future, where there are healers." She pushed her fingers deep into his thick hair and held onto him. "It took me three days before my memories returned, but once they did, I had everything. I came as soon as I could."

"I dinnae understand. Were you no' well?" He fiddled with the domes on her jeans until he snapped each one open.

"I'm just fine, and you're going to be a daddy."

"What?" He stopped and stared at her.

"That's exactly what I said when I first heard. It was the shock I needed for my memories to surge." She guided his hands to her waistband. "You're getting distracted. Jeans off now."

He peeled them down her legs and off. "I need to love you, as I did on our wedding night." His voice was a purr as he licked the skin along her inner thighs. "Say, aye."

"Yes, and I like your kind of loving. I will always wish for it." She pressed her hips toward him and a thrill chased through her. He stroked her flesh with his tongue and she clung to him, her pulse soaring. "And here's to wishes being granted."

"I love you, Lila." With the most intimate of kisses, he built her orgasm to a pinnacle until she clung to the most perilous edge. "Give in to me."

"No. I want you inside me."

"Aye, where we are one and none may tear us apart." He carried her to his bed, lowered her onto the brown fur covering and shucked his clothes. His cock, so thick and full, bobbed against his belly. "You're no' leaving me again."

Since she'd arrived before her first unsuccessful attempt at swimming the sound, she'd remain. She wouldn't repeat the past, not when it had all gone so terribly wrong.

"My father returns from Edinburgh in a few weeks. We'll figure out a way for me to see Nanna and meet him then." Mesmerized, she caressed his sculpted chest and his honed muscles rippled under her touch. She skated along the enticing path of his glorious abs then lower still, until she sank her fingers through his dark curls and cupped his balls. "Here I'll remain."

"Aye, together." His golden eyes smoldered as he traced one lone finger around her nipple. "If I must, I'll enter into talks with John MacIan."

He dipped his head and kissed her, his tongue sweeping over hers in a hot, languorous caress. Her body clenched so tight she almost came from his kiss alone. "You are going to make the perfect husband."

"Aye, my charm, until the end of time." He gripped her knees, spread her legs and thrust inside her with one powerful stroke.

The impact of their fast joining had her fighting to hold onto her control. She'd been bound to him throughout the centuries, and she'd never leave him again.

"Look at where we're joined." With slow deliberation, he

pulled out then pushed back in, the exquisite length of him scorching every nerve along her channel. "I love you, Lila. From the depths of my soul, all I have is yours."

He plunged into the very heart of her, and giving into her body's demands, she exploded with an array of spectacular colors erupting behind her closed eyelids. She soared, wrestling to draw breath as she came over and over. He was so deep, his roar of satisfaction echoing in her ears, and a more precious moment she'd never known.

They were joined in the most elemental of ways, she and her Highlander from another time.

* * * *

"Wake up, Lila." Calum caressed her bare back until she moaned and rolled toward him. They'd been abed for two days, but he'd slipped away at dawn to request Brother John meet them in the great hall at midday. For a small fee, he'd obtained a special license from the clergyman and they were set to wed. He just had to rouse his bride.

"What time is it?" She dislodged the white bed sheet as she lifted her arms and stretched. Do you have to return to your men?"

"Soon. For now, 'tis time to speak our vows." He traced around her belly's heart shaped mole where their bairn grew.

"We've already spoken those, and in the most unique way." Grinning, she shoved him onto his back, climbed over top and straddled his hips. "Although I'm up for that again if you are."

"Our next vows will be spoken afore the clan." He edged up onto his elbows and licked the peaking tips of her breasts bobbing so close to his mouth. "Will you do me the great honor of marrying me? I wish to keep my charm for all time."

"I'm getting an actual proposal?" She rubbed against his cock pressing eagerly against her warm entrance. "Then the answer's yes. I wish for a lifetime with you."

"Good. I wouldnae have accepted any other answer." He

cupped the back of her head and drew her mouth back to his.

Aye, she was his woman. His charm.

He'd keep her safe, always and forever.

Chapter 12

As soon as Calum left their cave, Lila snuck out and hurried along the narrow ledge. She searched the forest, then with all clear, jumped from the end to the soft sand, and barefoot, raced toward the loch.

A month ago, they'd spoken their vows before Brother John and their entire clan, and since, Colin had barely allowed her out of his sight.

"Lila, wait." Calum shot out from the trees and chased her, his white shirttails flying.

"I want to take a swim. I miss the sea." She snatched the fluttering ribbons of her cream gown and tried to unfasten the stays as she ran. "You can't keep me from the loch forever."

"Got you." He swung her into his arms.

"No. You are too fast for your own good." She slapped his chest. "What am I going to do with you?"

"I can tell you exactly what you should do." He strode along the water's edge. "We'll swim later, but together. Will that suffice?"

"I can swim without your supervision."

"The water's chilly." The waves rolled in, splashing her skirts and darkening the hems of his leather pants. Farther along the beach, a fire blazed within a small pit at the edge of the dunes as a final blaze of red seared the sunset sky. The rays lit Calum's golden eyes, turning them a smoldering hue as he set her down on the tartan spread before the fire. He eased in behind her, rested his chin on the top of her head.

"This is a beautiful spot." She tucked her skirts under her legs and embraced his warmth as the crashing waves rolled in.

They'd made so many new memories this past month. Calum had even taken her to the meadow of wildflowers. He was her destiny, and always would be.

It had been hard knowing Nanna was so close, that she was unable to see her, but here she'd remained. At least Calum had ensured the letter she'd written her had been received. His man had even waited for a response, and she kept her grandmother's note close, right in her pocket along with her charm.

"What has that worried look on your face?" With one arm wrapped around her, he caressed her belly, holding her and their child close.

"Nanna, John and Janet are arriving in another two days. I'm getting nervous."

"You've already met your father."

"Yes, but you and I are the only ones with memories from the time I traveled. I returned to the same moment I first had, and I've never been anywhere now but with you."

Since Margaret and Colin hadn't remembered her, she'd detailed everything in her letter to Nanna, telling her exactly what had happened. Nanna's answering letter had confirmed that she too hadn't recalled Lila's first journey through time. No memories. Not one of their reunion at Mingary.

Still, Nanna had reassured her she'd pave the way with her father, ensuring he knew her marriage to Calum was her choice. Nanna had written she held hope that another marriage between a MacLean and a MacIan might tip the scales toward finally cementing closer ties between their two clans. Instead of inflaming the feud, Lila might just be the one to calm it.

"John agreed to enter into talks with me. 'Tis a good start." Calum slid her hair to the side and nuzzled her neck. "I've received word too that Janet longs to see Margaret and her grandchildren. We'll begin working on a resolution, with or without the king's decree. While your MacIan kin are at Duart, I give you my word no harm shall come to them." He eased back, taking her with him to lie flat on the sand. "Do you trust me?"

"With my life." She rubbed her nose against his. "Nanna always said one day I would spread my wings and fly. I only wish to fly with you."

"Then allow me to see to that." He kissed her, long and with sensual seduction.

Her charm heated in her pocket, and she smiled against his lips.

Every moment with him now was hers to cherish forever.

Soar she would, and to the very stars.

* * * *

On her tiptoes, Lila tried to shove past Calum's broad back as they waited on Duart's sea-gate stone landing two days later. The MacIan's birlinn had berthed, and John, in a white tunic and leather pants, aided Nanna and Janet out as several of their warriors surrounded them. They were well armed, but no surprises there. Still, this was to be a peaceful visit, one that both Calum and her father had agreed to.

From beside her, Margaret, in a flurry of teal skirts, squealed and raced toward Janet. The two women cried and jumped in a dizzying circle.

Nanna, her black hair wisped with gray pinned high atop her head, waved to her, and Josiah bounded out and caught Nanna's arm to keep her steady on the landing. She looked healthy and happy in a burgundy gown with long lace tapered sleeves.

"Let me go, Calum."

"Aye, love." He kissed the top of her head then stepped aside. "Go and see your kin."

"Nanna!" She ran into her grandmother's open arms, and tears streaked down their cheeks. "I'm so glad you're here."

"I've been waiting forever to see you, my dear. I couldn't believe your letter said you'd already traveled through time, but it looks like that's been for the best. We're here, and that would never have happened otherwise. You have to tell me everything."

"I can't believe the secrets you kept from me as a child." She tapped Nanna's nose. "No more."

"Oh dear." She smiled mischievously. "I promise. No more. Just as well we don't have to have that conversation again. Come meet your father. It's past time." She turned and grasped John's arm. "John, this is your daughter, Lila."

"Aye, I hear we've already met." Eyes twinkling, he lifted her off her feet and swung her about. "I cannae believe I have a daughter. 'Tis a miracle you survived your birth, and most grateful I am for your grandmother's wish."

"Thank you for coming and agreeing to the talks."

"This feud must come to an end, and with you wed to a MacLean, I'll do all I can to ensure it is so." He cupped her face. "You have your grandmother's eyes, and those of a child born under a falling star."

"You said that the first time we met." She wiped her wet cheeks.

"A time I dinnae remember. Still, we have all the time in the world now. I will know you as I should have all these years."

Calum set a hand on her hip from behind and she eased back until she pressed against his chest. "Father, meet the man who has saved my life, and more times than I can count."

"It seems you have a penchant for saving lives, Calum. Mine, and now my daughter's." John extended his hand and Calum shook it. "I'm aware of what you've done from Lila's missive to my mother. You have my thanks."

"I'm glad you accepted my invitation to travel here. These talks are about negotiating peace, and you have my word you'll leave as you've arrived, safe and well."

"It's time to put this feud to rest. I want naught more than to see it come to an end, for my clan's sake, and my wife's as well. Janet misses her kin."

Nanna pulled her back into a hug and jiggled about. "I can't believe I'm going to be a great grandmother. I want to hear everything."

"Then I'll start again at the very beginning." She looped her arm through Nanna's and led her up the grassy incline toward Duart. Margaret and Janet walked behind them. Calum and John brought up the rear. This would be the end of the feud. She'd ensure it.

Oh, she had her grandmother back, and her father close.

Her future had been fully realigned, and the past set to rights.

No more traveling through time.

It was time to live.

Yes, and with the warrior who'd always been hers.

Author's Note

Restoration work began at the ruins of Mingary Castle in two-thousand and thirteen, and it's one day hoped the castle will be fully repaired.

For the purposes of this story, I chose to send Lila MacIan back to the year fifteen-hundred and ninety, because Sir Lachlan Mor MacLean, the fourteenth Chief of Clan MacLean of Duart, had been imprisoned by the king due to his feud with the MacDonald of Dunnyveg, his brother-in-law. The king did in fact induce all those involved in the dispute, being Donald MacDonald of Sleat, Angus MacDonald of Dunnyveg and Lachlan MacLean of Duart, to go to Edinburgh. When they each arrived, they were apprehended and imprisoned. I altered this event slightly, stating that the MacLean chief had been captured by the king's men to suit the story.

Lachlan MacLean's successor was his son Hector Og MacLean, a minor, and with someone needing to lead the clan, I chose Calum MacLean.

Calum MacLean and Lila MacIan are fictional characters.

This terrible feud between the clans raged for years. Both MacLean and MacDonald ravaged by fire and sword, laying waste to huge portions of each other's lands, and all within the

Western Isles were affected.

The account told of John MacIan of Ardnamurchan marrying Janet Campbell (Lachlan MacLean's mother) at Duart Castle in fifteen-hundred and eighty-eight, along with the subsequent massacre of eighteen of his attendants, and MacIan's imprisonment within Duart's dungeons for the year following it, was as accurate as I could convey it from the historical information on record of this event. Certainly nothing would persuade MacIan to join with Lachlan MacLean and ultimately go against his MacDonald kin during this great feud.

This story is woven with as much accuracy to the period and locations as possible, but any mistakes made are mine alone.

This book forms part of my *Highlander Heat* series, and each within it are stand-alone.

Please feel free to search for any of my other works. I simply adore strong heroines, and have a ton of fun matching them with their honorable alpha heroes.

Also available in paperback
Scottish Historical Romance

Traveling through time…for a Highlander.

Highlander Heat Series

Highlander's Castle, Book One

Highlander's Magic, Book Two

Highlander's Charm, Book Three

Highlander's Guardian, Book Four

Highlander's Faerie, Book Five

Highlander's Champion, Book Six

by Joanne Wadsworth

Looking for more sexy Scottish adventure?

Read on to catch a preview of the next book in the
Highlander Heat series.

Highlander's Guardian

Highlander Heat Book Four

by Joanne Wadsworth

Highlander's Guardian

Highlander Heat Series, Book Four

Chapter 1

Holyrood House, Edinburgh, 1590.

Tension tightened every muscle in Annie MacLeod's body as she hid behind a tree in the sprawling park near Holyrood House. Clutching the rough bark, she snuck a look around the wide trunk. Twenty feet away, one of her two guardians, Colin MacLean, paced a muddy track between two elm trees, his brow furrowed.

Of all the luck. She'd stumbled upon Colin in this secluded wooded area yesterday after he'd arrived at the king's palace. If he discovered her outside again without an adequate guard or chaperone, she'd be in twice the trouble. Aye, Colin would believe she was up to old tricks, following him as she'd done throughout her childhood.

Hands bunched in her thick burgundy skirts, she crept back a step and crunched on the thick matting of autumn leaves. Drat. Hardly needing to give her location away, she held perfectly still, then carefully, slowly, she slid her other foot back to join the other. No crunching.

Now, one step at a time and she'd escape without notice.

She eased back again, but her slipper sank into soggy soil at the edge of the trail. Precariously close to a thorny bush, she wobbled. When would she ever—

"Annie MacLeod," Colin growled as he came out of nowhere, gripped her waist and hauled her back to safety. "What are you doing in the middle of the forest without a guard, yet again?"

"Ah, I was walking, although apparently no' very well. Thank you for your aid." Her heart pounded and she covered his hands with hers. His fingers, so big and warm, splayed wide over her waist. Colin could move with such stealth and speed. "Please, dinnae tell Rory you've seen me."

"And why should I do that? Where's your aunt?"

"I didnae care to wake her, and Rory's so busy with the king. Interrupting him in order to ask for a guard wasnae something I wished to do."

"Then you should have interrupted me. I'm your guardian, just as Rory is."

"As you can see I did." She smiled, as sweetly as she could in the hope of diverting his attention. "In an indirect sort of way."

"'Tis just as well I heard you, and dinnae give me that sly smile of yours, you scamp."

She smiled wider. Colin may be her guardian, but he was also one of her nearest and dearest. "I couldnae help but notice how worried you looked. Is all well?"

"As well as can be considering my chief is in the cells." He released her and clasped one hand over the hilt of his side sword. The move stretched the fine silk of his black doublet over his broad chest. "Are you aware the MacDonalds of Skye arrived this morn? They remain a distinct threat against your MacLeod and my MacLean kin. You're no' to wander about like this again. If aught happened to you, I'd never forgive myself. Every precaution must be taken."

"The king will never allow the clans to fight while at

court." She touched the frown line slashing his brow and smoothed it out. "I hate to see you worry so."

"That does no' mean they willnae take their quarrels outside, and that is where we are."

"I needed some fresh air and time to think. It isnae easy trying to find a husband amongst the pomp of courtiers who are here." She'd been hounded of late. Like fresh meat to the market, they'd soon learnt she was here at Rory's bidding to choose a husband before the king did so for her, and not for the first time, but the second. Her first contracted handfast had failed, and once was enough. This time Rory had given her the choice to find a suitable match, a rare thing allowed for a woman and an offer she'd pounced on and accepted.

"If you wish aid in finding a husband, I'm here." Colin stroked a finger under her chin, his gaze softening and his touch comforting her. "You need only ask and I'll do whatever I can to help you."

"You're here for your chief and I cannae take you away from that duty." His chief had been captured by the king's men and tossed into Holyrood's tower for his part in the current feud between the clans. She'd been surprised to hear of it. Certainly a great chief like Lachlan MacLean didn't deserve to be treated so.

"I'm here for you as well, and we're kin."

Aye, their grandparents had been cousins, their mothers the closest of friends. On the Isle of Mull, she'd grown up traipsing around after Colin like an adoring child. He'd been so much older and wiser, the gap between them a wide six years, although now she'd turned one and twenty, that divide no longer seemed any great distance at all. "I miss roaming around Mull and being young and carefree. With you."

"Aye, our childhood is gone afore we know it, but since you're still successfully sneaking out after me, you're apparently missing very little." He grinned and her heart lightened at seeing his worry ease.

"I used to don a pair of your old breeches to make my escape less noticeable, but for some reason you always used to sense me nearby regardless." She'd idolized Colin, had missed him and his brother terribly when she'd left at three and ten for the Isle of Skye. Rory MacLeod, her chief and cousin, had requested her father's return to Dunvegan Castle upon Rory's eldest brother's death, and though her mother was a MacLean, her father was a MacLeod and had been honor bound to answer Rory's call-to-arms. Her father had joined Rory as the feud between them and the nearby MacDonald clan had escalated. "Just afore you said the MacDonalds had arrived. Whom exactly?"

"The MacDonald chief's nephews, James and Hugh, as well as a dozen of their warriors."

Not the best news, although not entirely unexpected. The MacDonald chief and his brother both resided in the tower along with Colin's chief. The king had captured each of three clan chiefs involved in the feud and demanded they enter into talks, albeit behind bars.

"Colin, I know James." As much as she detested the MacDonalds, James was different. James was the younger brother of the man the king had first ordered her to handfast with. In the sennight before she was supposed to speak her vows, she'd stayed at the MacDonald's stronghold and discovered James wished for peace, as greatly as she did. He'd been attentive and kind to her while she'd awaited his brother's return. As luck would have it, his brother had instead fallen in love and wed one of her kin with a close namesake, Anne MacLeod. His subsequent marriage to Anne had nullified their coming handfast and she'd been released to return to her MacLeod kin. "James was naught but kind to me while I stayed at Dunscaith Castle."

"Annie, all MacDonalds are a threat. You must no' become complacent around them."

Aye, anything she said right now in James's defense

wouldn't change Colin's opinion, particularly when she too detested the MacDonald chief. Donald MacDonald was a warrior who wanted it all, and if a clan stood in his way, he battled to remove them. Glad she was she'd never met him. "James is still different to his warmongering uncle, one of the few MacDonalds who is."

"The MacDonalds are all alike. Something you will learn in time." His golden eyes darkened and by his determined expression, his mind was clearly set. "I cannae believe Rory didnae send word to me of the king's handfast demand. That he would tie you to a MacDonald is despicable."

"He had no choice. The king forced his hand." Rory loathed the MacDonalds as much as Colin did, although Rory wished for peace and was willing to negotiate to a certain degree.

"I still should have been told. You're my ward, as much as you are Rory's."

"I asked him no' to tell you." She'd pleaded with Rory that he not send a missive to Colin on Mull. "Colin, your fury would have erupted and caused more problems than what I'd been attempting to solve. I was trying to bring about peace, no' escalate the war."

"The king still forces his wishes upon us. He needs to leave us alone to resolve our own issues, no' alter the way we settle our disputes." His pacing resumed as he tugged at his collar. "Even now, you're still being forced to find a husband when 'tis the last thing you wish."

"At least Rory has afforded me the choice, something I didnae have afore." Which so far had been of little more help. Since she'd arrived at the king's palace and begun her search, she'd been comparing every possible suitor to Colin. She wanted a man like him who would stand by her and her clan's side, caring for each and every one in turn. Even now his concern was etched heavily on his face. "You would make a wonderful husband. Have you ever thought of taking a wife?"

"I war too much."

"Aye, and you also argue too much." She couldn't help the tease.

"Arguing is good for the soul."

"A wife is also good for the soul."

A smile lifted his lips. "I fear, I would only argue with her as well."

"She would need to be rather resilient." She caught his hands, his palms warm against hers and hopping backward, tugged him along the path. "Let's walk afore the day is done. Then you may argue with me some more. I know how much you enjoy that."

"A walk would be good, and watch your step, Annie." He turned her around, slid her hand through his crooked arm and guided her down the trail that led deeper into the woods. "I've missed you and your liveliness."

"I've missed you too." The foliage above thickened, blocking what little remained of the late afternoon sunshine, but Colin's solid presence warmed her through as it always did. "Last month your visit to Dunvegan Castle was so short. We didnae even get to speak."

"I'm sorry about that, scamp." He squeezed her hand, his voice tender as he used her childhood nickname. "I had only a few hours to spare afore I had to return to Duart Castle."

"Is that when your chief was first captured?"

"Aye, and we expected the MacDonalds to attack with their full force upon hearing the news. That was why I came to Dunvegan, to seek Rory's aid and some additional men for the battle, only I discovered from him both the MacDonald of Sleat and the MacDonald of Dunnyveg too had been captured by the king's men. Rory confirmed the two MacDonald clans were in as much turmoil as ours by the loss of their chiefs." He stepped ahead and held up a low branch so she could pass through. "Come, less about my problems when I need to consider yours.

If you wish aid in finding a husband, then allow me to see who's at court this eve and consider any possible prospects."

"Elizabeth has introduced me to almost every unmarried man since I arrived, even Lord Sinclare who must be at least seventy." She rolled her eyes, not impressed at all that she had to consider a man who needed two canes to walk stably with.

"You mean old Batten-face Sinclare is a possible suitor?" He chuckled and she slapped his arm.

"Dinnae laugh. I have no desire to be that man's wife."

"Ah, but consider the benefits. He'd have years of wisdom to offer you."

"Aye, but no' years to give it. When he and I spoke, he made it quite clear he's here to find a young wife in order to provide him with an heir since both his sons passed. I do feel sorry for him, but no' enough to accept a proposal."

"His sons perished in a battle that took many lives. They were good men. I knew them." Colin withdrew his sword and slashed a thorny bush blocking the thin path before stepping through. "We're almost there."

"Almost where?" Birds twittered from their nests above, the forest so thick that nothing but the trees surrounded them.

"On a past trip, I discovered this loch, though 'tis well hidden." Colin returned to her, bent and brushed a soft kiss against her forehead. "Look ahead. I've cleared the way."

He stepped aside and she gasped.

The loch was small, private and completely hidden, its glassy surface dancing with the reflection of the towering trees encircling it. "'Tis beautiful."

"And all ours. How about we have some fun? Like old times."

"You hardly need to ask." His form of fun spoke to her heart and always had. She skipped to the water's edge, lifted her skirts and knelt on the spongy moss. With her hands cupped, she dipped them into the clear water and sipped. "Is this place completely secluded?"

"You wish to swim?"

"You know I do." He'd been able to read her mind for years. She loosened the ties of her burgundy jacket, slipped it off her shoulders and laid it overtop a boulder. "Will you come too?"

"Aye, I can wear my tunic." Turning, he gave her his broad back.

"Thank you for bringing me here. This is exactly what I needed." He'd always been able to ease her worries as none other could. She unlaced her gown's front stays and shed it along with her stockings, leaving her sark as adequate coverage. Then with care, tugged the pins from her hair and swished her head from side to side and released the long golden length. "Do you feel better too?"

"I always do around you, my wee scamp." He divested himself of his weapons, a sword and dirk before shrugging off his doublet. His dark hair wisped with blond ends brushed his shoulders as he bent and hauled off his boots.

She should avert her gaze, but she wasn't nearly as chivalrous as Colin. Instead, as he shucked his leather trews and his white tunic fluttered against him mid-thigh, she smiled with appreciation at the sight of his muscled legs. "Oh, Colin, I'm having the most scandalous thoughts."

"Are you watching me?" He glanced over his shoulder and sighed, rather raggedly. "You're looking for trouble with that kind of expression on your face."

"I'm sorry, but I couldn't help myself. Let's swim." Smiling, she rolled her sark's thin ivory cotton sleeves to the elbow. At the bank's edge, she dove into the pool and almost lost her breath at the frigid impact with the water. 'Twas beyond cold, but still refreshingly so. After breaking the surface, she treaded water and called, "'Tis wonderful, and you're missing out."

With his gaze on hers, he advanced. "I believe the last time we swam together would have been in the loch near my old tree hut."

"Aye, that's right." It had been a year since she'd last visited Colin and her mother's kin at Duart Castle on Mull. Colin had skipped his afternoon duties one day and taken her down to the sea. Together they'd swum, him powering through the water with such skilled ease and she being as sly as she could to keep up.

"Bet I can still catch you. Swim. Fast." He flashed a smile full of challenge, then ran and dove.

A wave rippled toward her. She ducked her head, tossed her feet into the air and went under. Kicking toward the center of the pool, she remained below, her lungs near to bursting. Surely, he'd think she'd—

A hand clamped around her ankle and Colin dragged her upward.

She broke the surface in a slew of bubbles and gulped in great breaths.

"Too easy. That white sark you're wearing is like a flag under the water." His gaze was wolfish, his hands on her hips sending a thrill through her.

"Then close your eyes as you should have afore you dove in. Give me time to get away." She shoved a wave of water at him.

He fell back, shook his dark head and sent a spray of drops flying. "So that's how 'twill be."

"Always."

"I'll give you a minute head-start to hide." He lunged and she squealed and kicked backward. "Starting now. One." He closed his eyes.

She was off, kicking with fast strokes toward the stone ledge at the far end. If she could climb on top then she'd be able to hide where it dipped out of sight to the side. He'd never look for her out of the water.

Her sark swirled around her legs, hindering her a touch when she usually only wore an old shirt in the water, but still, she should be able to make that ledge before her minute was up.

"Sixty," Colin yelled.

"Nay, you cheated." He'd counted to ten and no more. She was certain of it.

His golden eyes shone with laughter as he caught up and passed her. She nabbed his feet and held on. Using his arms alone, he powered them both the last twenty feet to the wide overhanging ledge. Then with his hands on the rock, he hauled himself up, reached down and lifted her onto the flat stone beside him. "You've always been a tricky lass. Were you going to hide up here?"

"How could you even think I would?" Water dripped from her dangling feet into the loch.

"Because I know you too well." He caught her hand and pressed it against his thumping heartbeat. "Spending such time with you is always tiring."

"Yet you love it." He'd been her closest kin growing up, and they'd had so much fun, no matter the years separating them. Gently, she spread her fingers over his solid muscle. His wet shirt, almost transparent, showed a smattering of dark chest hair. She slid one finger into the gap between two loosened ties and as his muscles flexed under her touch, a strange heat surged through her.

Now she'd touched him, she couldn't stop, and since he hadn't moved to halt her, she trailed her finger down over each of his rigid abs and swished along his trim waist. Oh, being this close to him was glorious. New and needy emotions reared to life within her. She wanted, and more.

* * * *

Colin's heartbeat thumped as Annie's blue eyes darkened and her breathing quickened. Her wet sark was pressed against her chest, showing the roundness of her full breasts and a tease of pink nipple. The sight sent wicked thoughts racing through his mind, although thoughts he wasn't permitted to have.

He closed his eyes, shoved what he'd seen into the darkest recesses of his mind then opened his eyes and grabbed her wayward hand. She was his ward, and had been since her father had passed away three years ago. "Annie, stop."

"Please, no' yet." She wriggled her fingers free and let them drift over his belly.

"We're cousins." Damn it. He had to stop her before she encountered his rising cock.

"Nay, our grandparents were cousins. We're far removed from being first cousins."

"Third cousins still shouldnae touch each other so."

"Then you might like to inform the king, because there's currently no law against it."

Ever since she'd lost her parents, she'd sought comfort from him on a greater level, and he'd done all he could to provide whatever she'd needed. Except she was no longer a child and as her guardian, he had a responsibility to ensure her future was secured. To the right man, and that would never be him when he had to lead his clan during this current feud. Aye, he needed to push her away, except they'd always been so close, their bond one he adored. Hurting her was impossible. Tenderly, he caught her face in his hands, traced his thumbs over the dusting of freckles covering her tiny nose and cheeks. "I'm no' the man for you, but I will aid you in searching for one. Tell me what you're looking for in a husband."

"In truth, I'd like someone just like you." She skimmed her hands over his. "I'd also love to return to my MacLean roots and be closer to you and my kin. If you're adamant there is naught between us, then I would like a man from Mull."

"You dinnae wish a husband of rank? You can only find that here at court."

"Rank means little when it is what's inside a person that counts." She released him and tapped her chin. "Hmm, what of Arthur?"

"My second isnae looking for a wife when the last lass who took his fancy married another." A small lie, but he'd never be able to stand aside and watch his right-hand man wed her. "He's also here to aid me, no' to woo the lasses."

"Of course. I'm sorry. How long until the king approves your request for a visit with Lachlan? You said yesterday you were waiting."

"That all depends on how accommodating the king is. With the feuds raging, he has little patience with the MacLeans."

"Then you need to be careful and no' aggravate him. I dinnae want you being thrown behind bars right along with your chief."

"I'll be careful, but should I end up in the cells, I expect you to come and visit me."

A teasing smile lifted her lips. "I guess I could bring you your daily bread and water."

"Imp." He swung her into his arms and tossed her into the loch with a resounding splash.

She came up spluttering and laughing, her waist-length hair floating like a lily pad of white-blond around her. "Are you using your strength against me again, Colin MacLean?"

"You need to learn when to hold your tongue."

"I was trained to banter at a very young age, and by the very best. You." Her gaze traveled down his body and she gasped.

Hell. He plucked his wet shirt from his groin, but his stiffened cock was still easy to see. Just when he'd diverted her mind, now he'd gone and brought her thoughts roaring right back on him.

"Colin?" She jerked forward, swam to the ledge and held out her arms for him to lift her up. "Please."

Why couldn't she be like the other lasses and more reserved in her manner? An interrogation was sure to come. He hunkered down, gripped her hands and lifted her. Gently, he set her on her feet beside him as he remained standing. "I want you to forget what you just saw."

"I should, but…" She swayed closer, grazing his chest with her hard nipples. "If you feel aught toward me then we need to speak of it."

"Nay, I feel naught but the love of one cousin for another." His heart ached at the mistruth, but speaking honestly on this subject would do neither of them any good, not when he'd chosen to live by his sword as the captain of his chief's guard. She deserved far more than a warrior whose death might come at any time.

"Do you truly speak the truth? I willnae abide any lies between us."

"Neither will I, and I've no reason to lie to you." And now 'twas time to end this conversation before things between them led down an irreversible path. He strode along the ledge toward the bank. "'Twill be dark soon and we need to return afore you're missed. Should Rory discover you've left the palace on your own, he'll send out a search party."

"Nay, he'll know I'm with you." She chased after him. "I'm no' done talking with you, Colin."

"What we need to do is to find you a man who can handle your constant need to talk." He bounded onto the grassy bank and held out his hands. "Jump."

She did and he caught and swung her down next to him. "Stop jesting with me."

"I'll aid you this eve in finding the right man." He led her to her clothes then dressed as quickly as he could. "It willnae be an easy task, but I'll manage it, somehow."

"You are a stubborn man, third cousin of mine." She wrung her hem then donned her burgundy gown and jacket over top of her wet underclothes.

"Thank you." He ran his fingers through her long locks, tidying her hair as best he could.

"That wasnae a compliment, you dolt." She grasped her skirts and tramped back down the thin forest trail toward the palace.

Hell, he desperately wanted to drag her into his arms and see what their future could possibly hold, but instead he allowed her to walk ahead until they emerged from the woods and the thick stone walls of Holyrood House rose like an impenetrable fortress in the descending dark.

Ahead of him, Annie hastened toward the two-story gatehouse where battlements topped fortified walls and guardsmen patrolled the barbican. Beyond the arch, the north-west tower housing King James VI's apartments rose high and overlooked all. The king who'd imprisoned his chief, and the king he sought an audience with.

He caught Annie up, and with a hand on her lower back, steered her across the inner courtyard toward the side entrance near the service quarters. 'Twas best they bypassed the great hall and surrounding rooms which would be abuzz with people so close to the dinner hour. The less people who saw their damp hair and clothing, the better.

Annie slipped through the open doors and peeked down the corridor. "'Tis clear. I didnae realize 'twas so late. Aunt Elizabeth will have already left her chamber and joined the guests for the evening meal."

"Then we'll change quickly and find her." He led her down the gloomy passageway lit by the odd candle in an iron wall sconce. Along the darkest section, he stopped outside her paneled door next to her aunt's chamber and nodded at her. "I'll wait here."

Annie tipped her ear up. "I hear something."

The heavy clomp of booted feet traveled toward him.

Quickly, he nudged her out of sight into the recessed alcove beside her door. "Shh," he whispered in her ear. "No' a noise."

"I cannae believe you lost track of the MacLeod chit in the woods. I gave you one simple task, to follow her," a man rasped as he stormed past them with another man, their tall, shadowed bodies blending into the dark.

"I watched her for a mite," the other man said, "until she stumbled upon MacLean and the two vanished into the woods. I couldnae find where either of them had gone."

"Are they talking about me?" Annie hushed as she slid her hands around his waist and tucked her head under his chin.

"Aye." Colin wrapped his arms around her as the men disappeared around the far corner. "This is what I've been warning you about. Your cousin is the Chief of MacLeod. Not only is he deeply favored by the king, but any alliance formed with you brings with it Rory's might." Frustration burned through him. "Did you recognize their voices?"

"Nay." She stared down the corridor. "And 'twas too dark to see. You should follow them, discover who they are. There's time if you hurry."

"I cannae leave you alone after what I just heard. If there is one man seeking you, there could well be another. All here are aware you seek a husband." He opened her door and stopped in the pitch black. "Why has your maid has no' lit your fire or a candle?"

"I told her that could wait until I retired for bed. I thought I'd be back in plenty of time to dress afore it got dark."

"Wait here. I'll find us some light." He strode down the hallway to the last lit candle, collected it and returned. Annie stood shivering and rubbing her chilled arms. He set the candle in the holder on her side table and ushered her across to her curtained ambry. "Choose something warm and change, as quickly as you can."

"Is your tunic drying out, or will you need another for the

evening meal?" She selected a pale blue gown and stepped behind the silk dressing screen next to her four-poster bed with its sweeping navy velvet canopy and golden tassels.

"I'll need to change." Although, he wouldn't be leaving her alone, not after what he'd heard in the hallway. "We'll stay together."

"When the maid returned with my laundry this morn, by accident she left one of Rory's tunics behind. Rory will never know if you wish to borrow it. It'd save you a trip to your chamber."

"Aye, I'd appreciate it." Changing here would be far more preferable than having to sneak her to his wing which housed so many of the single men.

"You'll find his tunic on top of my trunk under the window."

"I see it." He tugged off his shirt, donned the white tunic and retied his black doublet.

"It appears I shall need a hand." Annie stepped out from behind the screen holding her gown's low-cut silk neckline to her chest. The full swell of her breasts rose on a deep inhale as she turned and gave him her back. Over her shoulder, she smiled. "You dinnae mind?"

"I'm no maid but I'll manage." Bare skin, so creamy and smooth, beckoned. He brushed aside her glossy blond locks, picked up the ties and laced the stays as quickly as he could. Finished, he ran her comb through her hair until the pale strands curled around his fingers like a silken web. "You're presentable."

Now they needed to go. His desire for her deepened with each moment they spent together, something he couldn't allow.

Finding her a husband was imperative, and soon.

* * * *

Annie wandered down the passageway, Colin at her side and his crisp outdoor scent swirling around her, a delectable tease of pine and fresh water she'd always adored.

"What has that smile on your face?" He pressed a hand to her lower back and warm tingles raced across her skin.

"Thoughts of you." If only she had more time to choose a husband, but Rory expected her to secure an engagement before they left Holyrood.

"You shouldnae be thinking of me." Colin stopped at the entrance to the great hall.

She took a deep, fortifying breath. The massive vaulted room held a sweeping crown of rafters rising to an impressive height more similar to a small cathedral. Beautiful tapestries, of hunting and landscape scenes, hung with pride around the vast room filled with a merry and hungry crowd. "Well, finding Aunt Elizabeth and Rory in this gathering willnae be an easy task."

"But find them we will. Come." Colin weaved around the perimeter and she followed in his path around the mingling groups. A serving girl approached with a tray and he accepted two goblets of wine, handed her one then continued on through the doors leading into a side room where pipers played a lively tune.

Music flowed around her as she sipped. "Can you see them?"

"Nay, no' yet. Mayhap we should eat afore attempting a more in-depth search." He stopped before a side table with a white embroidered tablecloth fluttering in the breeze from the open balcony doors. The table was laden with platters of meat and succulent roasted vegetables. Colin set his goblet down and selected a sugared plum, one of her favorite fruits. "Try this." He slipped it between her lips.

The sweet ripeness burst over her tongue and she licked his trailing fingertip, not wanting to miss a drop of the delicious juice. "Mmm, wonderful."

He groaned and cleared his throat. "Next time you can feed yourself."

She grinned. "All I heard was next time."

"Good evening." Arthur, Colin's right-hand man, eased past a group of guests and joined them. Wearing a forest-green silk tunic and black leather trews, the striking colors matched his vivid green gaze and midnight-black hair to perfection. "Annie, you're looking bonny this eve."

"Thank you. And you look dangerously dashing."

"Ah, lass, you'll make me blush." He took her hand and pressed a kiss against her knuckles.

"Enough." Colin knocked Arthur's shoulder. "No dallying with Annie when you're still distressed about the lass you lost."

"What lass is that?" Arthur frowned, his expression perplexed.

Oh, Colin had been telling fibs again. Well, two could play at that game. She set her goblet down and faced Arthur. The warrior stroked the hilt of his belted sword and the blade swayed and glinted in the candlelight. Aye, Arthur appealed, and she'd always felt so protected whether he or Colin were nearby. Certainly the man's towering height and powerful bearing showcased the depth of his MacLean ancestry, that of their Gaelic clan born of a king. Arthur had also always had a kind word for her. "How have you been of late, Arthur?"

"Better if our chief were no' locked behind bars."

Colin rested his hand on her lower back, stroked his thumb in a small circle. "Aye, I'm still awaiting word on when I may see Lachlan, but I hope soon."

Unable to help herself, she inched closer to Colin. His little touches always soothed her. "Why is the king taking so long to approve a visit?"

"He inserts his control, and none may gainsay him." Colin eyed his man. "We've been looking for Rory and Elizabeth. Have you by chance seen either of them this eve?"

"I passed Elizabeth only a moment ago." He motioned over Annie's shoulder toward a group of chattering women.

Her aunt's back was to her, but her unmistakable auburn hair, piled high atop her head, gave proof 'twas her. "Oh, how did I miss her?" She squeezed Colin's arm. "Stay and talk to Arthur. I willnae be long. I must see my aunt so she knows I've arrived."

"A sound idea. Save your first dance for me."

"I will." She clutched her skirts and eased around the dancers toward Elizabeth.

"Well, well, if it isnae Annie MacLeod." James MacDonald, attired in a great plaid fastened across his chest with a silver pin, stepped directly into her path. "You're the very lass I was after."

"James, how are you?" She fluttered her hand over her chest. Goodness, should Colin see her with his greatest enemy, a battle would certainly ensue.

"I'm well, but you've not yet been to Dunscaith Castle to see Anne." He crossed his arms and lifted one bushy red eyebrow. "My brother's new wife misses you."

"As I miss Anne, but I thought it best to give her some time to settle into her new home and married life afore I asked Rory if a visit might be permissible." Something she had no idea how she'd arrange when the relationship between their clans was so on edge. A truce had been achieved by the marriage of one of her kin, Anne MacLeod to Alex MacDonald, but 'twas still a very uneasy truce. "How is Anne?"

"Enjoying wedded bliss, as is my brother. 'Tis why I've come to Holyrood House in Alex's stead. Tearing him away from his wife right now would be impossible."

With Donald, his chief and uncle, currently in the cells, James would also be here for the same reason as Colin, to see his laird. Certainly no warrior left his chief to fight his battles alone.

"I'm also here because you are, Annie."

"Pardon?"

"Word reached me on Skye that you'd traveled to court to

seek a husband. Is the king still demanding you make a significant match?" Dozens of candles in the circular overhead chandelier highlighted the spark of interest in Donald's eyes.

"Aye, but this time the choice is mine, a wish Rory granted me." She and James had spoken honestly with each other during her short stay at Dunscaith.

"I'm glad." He glanced over her head and snorted. "Colin MacLean appears rather disturbed we're talking. It might pay for us to take this conversation to where we cannae be interrupted. Would you care to dance?"

"I was just on my way to see my—"

"Wonderful." He swung her onto the floor as a new reel started.

"James, what are you doing?"

"Proving that not all the MacDonalds and MacLeods enjoy warring. Smile, otherwise MacLean will take my head off if he thinks you didnae wish to join me."

"You're playing with fire." Still, she didn't intend to be the catalyst for Colin calling James out, so she planted a smile on her face and curtsied as another couple joined them and they formed a small circle.

"I like fire, but I also like a woman with spirit, and that trait you have in abundance." He caught her hands and moved her through the steps to the energetic tune.

A low growl sounded from close behind and she shivered as Colin made his displeasure more than known. To James, she whispered, "You'd best speak of what's on your mind afore the song ends."

"There is naught like a little rivalry to light a fire under a MacLean." He grinned, clearly enjoying himself.

"James." She wanted to slap him. "Speak now, or I shall leave you on this floor to fend off Colin on your own."

He chuckled but nodded. "Aye, you and I have always enjoyed each other's company which is unusual for those within our warring clans, and it's that friendship that now leads me to what I'd like to ask of you. Annie, if you're in need of a proposal, then I'd like you to consider forming an alliance with me. I realize you never wished to wed my brother, but 'tis time for me to take a wife and a marriage between the two of us would further strengthen the ties between our clans. When Anne wed Alex, it helped ease some of the immediate tension, but these are difficult times and unless the clans join more fully together, further unrest will only prevail."

Had he just proposed to her in the middle of the dance floor?

"Lass, dinnae look so shocked." He twirled her around and sent her pale blue skirts flying. "All I ask is that you take some time to consider my proposal, and while you do, allow me to court you. I simply ask for a fair chance at your hand."

Could she marry James? Aye, he'd been kind and considerate to her during her stay at the MacDonald stronghold while awaiting her handfast to his brother at the king's demand, and their friendship had remained strong since, but he was still Colin's enemy. "I'm no' sure."

Concern furrowed his brow. "Have you received another offer?"

"Nay."

"Then allow me to court you."

"That would be as good as saying aye to your proposal since a courtship usually leads to an engagement."

"Yet you must procure an engagement while you're here."

"An alliance has still been made between our clans because of Anne. She is a MacLeod and married to your brother."

"Anne has no direct tie to Rory, only you do. There is also the fact your mother was a MacLean. With both you and Anne living at Dunscaith Castle, there will finally be a chance for this feud to ease between all three clans. 'Tis time for the MacDonalds, MacLeods and MacLeans to cease fighting. Help me bring a resolution to all the years of fierce warring. Between you and I, we could do so."

She couldn't deny the truth in his statement, and marrying for such a reason would be an honorable thing to do. "You're quite serious?"

"Very." He grinned. "On the morrow, come riding with me. We shall speak more then."

"I would like that." Colin wouldn't, but then her choices were so limited.

"I'll meet you at the stables after you've had time to break your fast." He dipped his head.

"Aye, on the morrow."

"Thank you for agreeing." He pressed a kiss to her hand and walked away.

"What the hell did James want?" Colin rasped as he slid in behind her, his chest a solid wall of heat at her back.

"Dinnae be angry." She spun around.

"Speak. I'll have no secrets between us."

"He wishes to form an alliance and build the bonds between our clans."

"What kind of an alliance?" His golden eyes burned with fury.

"Surely you can imagine considering the reason why I'm here."

"He intends to offer for you?"

"Aye, he made his position clear."

"And so will I." He leaned in until his nose brushed hers. "You're no' to go near him again, and I will make certain of it. Do we understand each other?"

She surely did, but perhaps Colin had forgotten she had a mind of her own.

"Damn it. You're no' listening. I can see that defiant spark in your eyes. We need to talk, and somewhere where we'll be afforded more privacy." He guided her through the balcony doors and into the cool night air.

Aye, they would talk, and she didn't doubt this was one conversation she wouldn't care for.

Highlander Heat

Highlander's Castle, Book One
Highlander's Magic, Book Two
Highlander's Charm, Book Three
Highlander's Guardian, Book Four
Highlander's Faerie, Book Five
Highlander's Champion, Book Six

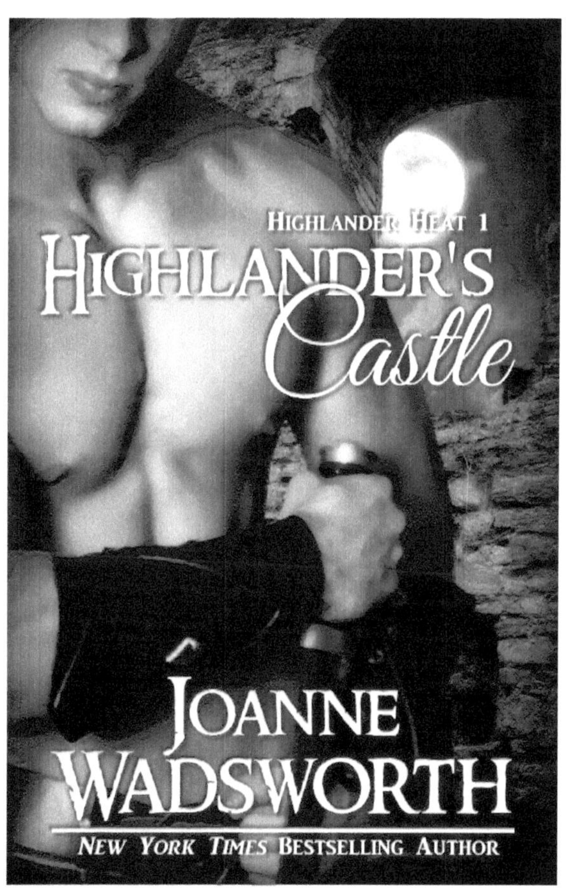

JOANNE WADSWORTH

The Matheson Brothers Continued

Highlander's Kiss, Book Four
Highlander's Heart, Book Five
Highlander's Sword, Book Six

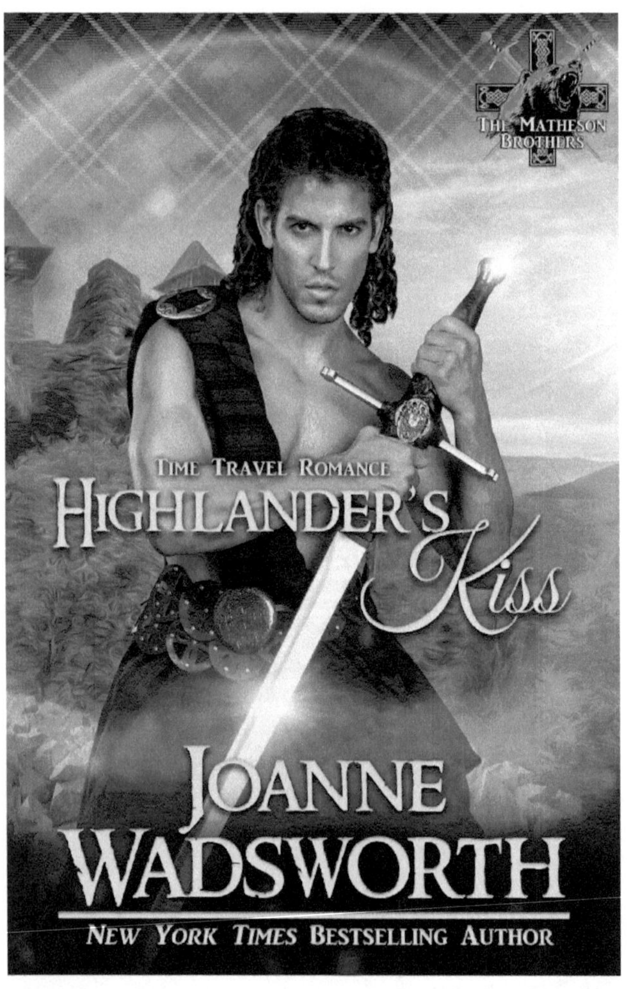

The Matheson Brothers Continued

Highlander's Bride, Book Seven
Highlander's Caress, Book Eight
Highlander's Touch, Book Nine

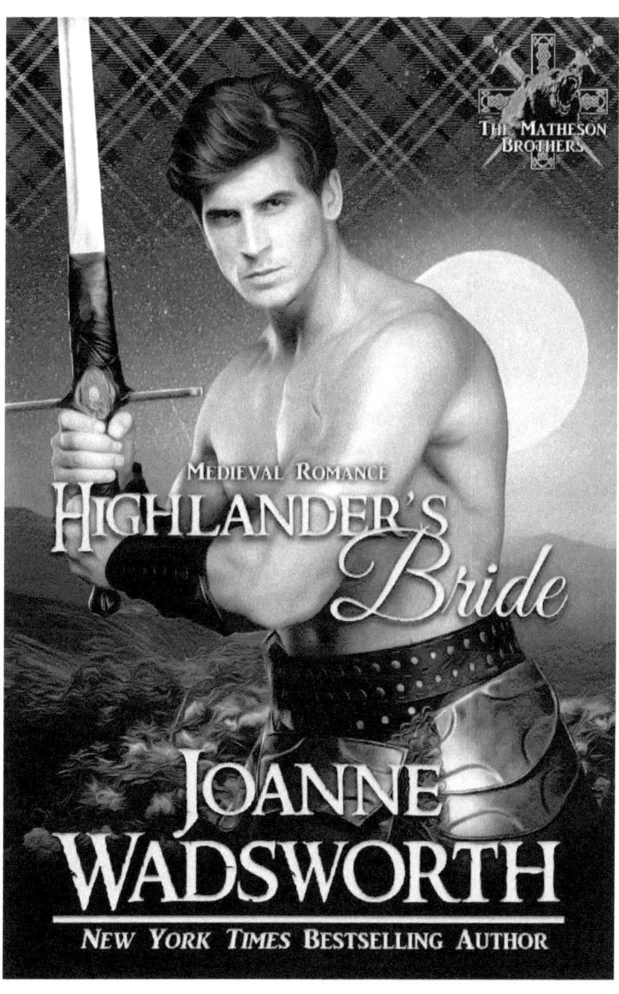

The Matheson Brothers Continued

Highlander's Shifter, Book Ten
Highlander's Claim, Book Eleven
Highlander's Courage, Book Twelve
Highlander's Mermaid, Book Thirteen

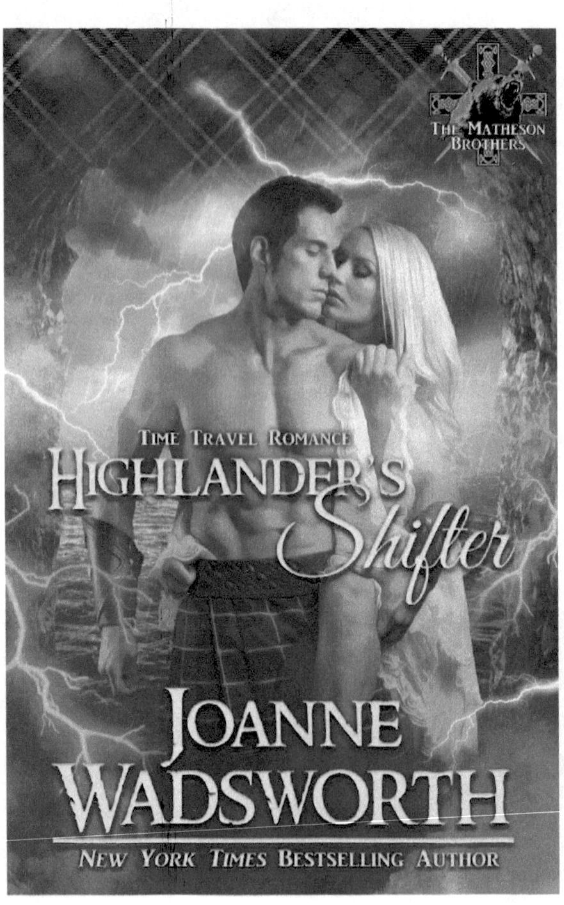

Princesses of Myth

Protector, Book One
Warrior, Book Two
Hunter (Short Story - Included in Warrior, Book Two)
Enchanter, Book Three
Healer, Book Four
Chaser, Book Five

BILLIONAIRE BODYGUARD
Attraction
BILLIONAIRE BODYGUARDS BOOK ONE
JOANNE WADSWORTH
NEW YORK TIMES BESTSELLING AUTHOR

JOANNE WADSWORTH

Joanne Wadsworth is a *New York Times* and *USA Today* Bestselling Author who adores getting lost in the world of romance, no matter what era in time that might be. Hot alpha Highlanders hound her, demanding their stories are told and she's devoted to ensuring they meet their match, whether that be with a feisty lass from the present or far in the past.

Living on a tiny island at the bottom of the world, she calls New Zealand home. Big-dreamer, hoarder of chocolate, and addicted to juicy watermelons since the age of five, she chases after her four energetic children and has her own hunky hubby on the side.

So come and join in all the fun, because this kiwi girl promises to give you her "Hot-Highlander" oath, to bring you a heart-pounding, sexy adventure from the moment you turn the first page. This is where romance meets fantasy and adventure…

To learn more about Joanne and her works, visit
http://www.joannewadsworth.com